THE APPROACHING STORM . . .

D avey was convinced that the Utes broke off the attack not out of fear, but because they had already demonstrated that they could win the fight with only a small number of warriors. For days now, their warriors had been signaling to their brothers to come to the mountains and gather for a big powwow. Those prospectors on Cherry Creek did not know what they would encounter in the Ute camp.

Davey was sure that if the white men attacked the camp, they would not find a mere dozen or so warriors, but an entire tribe of seasoned fighters. The Utes did not camp near noisy streams, but on high ground, well away from water. Long before the whites reached the Ute camp, the tribe would know they were going to be attacked.

And they would be waiting.

RIVERS
WEST

THE
SOUTH PLATTE

Jory Sherman

BANTAM BOOKS

NEW YORK • TORONTO • LONDON • SYDNEY • AUCKLAND

THE SOUTH PLATTE

A Bantam Book / September 1998

ISBN 0-553-56799-3

Published simultaneously in the United States and Canada

Bantam Books are published by Bantam Books, a division of Bantam
Doubleday Dell Publishing Group, Inc. Its trademark, consisting of the
words "Bantam Books" and the portrayal of a rooster, is Registered in
U.S. Patent and Trademark Office and in other countries. Marca
Registrada. Bantam Books, 1540 Broadway, New York, New York 10036.

PRINTED IN THE UNITED STATES OF AMERICA

OPM   10 9 8 7 6 5 4 3 2 1

THE
SOUTH PLATTE

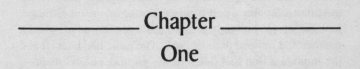

Chapter
One

Davey Longworth dropped the bale of furs when he heard the mule scream. The sound, so startling, shrill and rippled with terror, sent a chill up his spine. He kicked the makeshift fur press aside and reached for his rifle, which was propped up on one of the panniers, and cocked it as he drew it toward him. He heard the loud thud of something heavy falling and striking the earth. It came from downslope, from the general locale of the place where he had built winter quarters for the mules under an outcropping of rock.

His horse, a dun with four black stockings, which he had saddled earlier that morning, murmured a low whicker. The gelding's ears twitched and twisted like twin cones. "Rocky," Davey said in a soothing tone. The horse looked at his master with wide, fear-struck eyes, then whickered again and pawed at the partly frozen earth with its right front hoof.

Craggy peaks towered above Davey's camp, their high reaches still mantled in deep snow. They looked like ancient fortifications, ringing him in, keeping strangers out, throwing a mighty shadow over hundreds of acres like a shawl. In some places up there, Davey knew, summer never came, and there had not been a spring for centuries, only constant cold, ice, and buried secrets.

The first thing Davey thought was that a cougar had attacked one of the mules, but he had not heard a mountain lion's cough or any growling. Nor did he hear any other sound as stillness lay like a pall of white smoke on the air. Strange, he thought. He had only heard a mule scream once, when a panther had jumped onto its back. The mule had bucked and the mountain lion had fallen to the ground, behind its prey. The mule had kicked the lion senseless before the cat realized it was in trouble and had bounded away, with half an ear torn off and a sore leg. But this scream had sounded different, more shrill, and abruptly cut off.

Davey stepped away from the bales of fur and the panniers, the rope lashings all laid out for packing onto the mules, and found cover in the nearby firs and spruce, a place where he could not be seen easily. He waited, listening for any other sound, but after several seconds had gone by and he had heard nothing, he let out his breath. The warm spring sun glared down from a cloudless blue sky. The only sounds were the drip of melting snow from the needles of the tall pines and the swish of small rivers from under the spruce and fir.

It had been a long, hard winter, but he had done well with the beaver, the marten and mink, and he needed both mules to carry some of the furs to Cherry Creek, where the fur buyer from Bent's Fort would be waiting now that spring had begun to creep into the Rocky Mountains. He had already cached the better part of his catch and this was the day he had chosen to follow the Cache de la Poudre down the mountain and follow the South Platte along the foothills before heading east to the creek.

Davey stepped from the shadows and headed downslope toward the mules' shelter, stopping every few feet to listen for any alien sound and hearing only the slow drip of melted snow. The eerie silence was agonizing, for Davey knew that something had happened to one of the mules. There should have been other noises from the same direction, but there were none.

Davey came up behind the outcropping and stopped to listen again. He heard the mules moving around and that puzzled him. He could not see them until he stepped out of the forest. But what lay beyond, in the open? He didn't know, but he could feel his pulse hammering in his ears and there were flutters in his stomach that were the harbingers of fear, telling him something was wrong.

He had laid out fodder for the mules the night before, grasses he had cut from around the beaver ponds and hauled down on a travois, enough food to fill their bellies but not leave them sluggish in the morning. He could hear the mules nibbling on the grasses and snuffling as they tore off chunks of grass and munched them. But how many mules? He had three. One of them had screamed only moments before. Had a fight broken out over the food? Perhaps one of the mules had been kicked and hurt. But the scream had not sounded natural. No, something had happened to one of the mules and it hadn't been from a sound kick. That much he was sure of.

Davey circled the outcropping. He had taken only a few steps when he saw the overhanging rock and one of the mules standing hip-shot, staring at the ground. Gazing down, he saw another mule lying a few yards away, outside the rope-and-pine barrier he had erected from small trees only two to three inches thick. He sucked in a breath and steeled himself to step out into the open.

Looking all around, Davey stepped quickly to the edge of the corral. All three of his mules were inside the enclosure. They did not seem ruffled. It was as if nothing untoward had happened. But there on the ground lay a dead mule, its throat slit open, its mouth gaping, filled with dirt and stone. Davey quickly gulped in air to keep from vomiting. The mule's eyes had been gouged out and lay next to its body like a hideous pair of deformed hen's eggs. He felt a thrill of electricity shoot up his spine and the tiny hairs on the back of his neck bristled. He had gooseflesh on his arms as he knelt down and examined the butchered animal.

The mule had a white star on its forehead, a smallish blaze that was ragged around the oval edges. Davey peeled back the mule's upper lip and looked at its yellowed teeth. They were worn down, as he would have expected an eight-year-old's to be, but more on one side than the other. The slash in the animal's neck was vicious. The blade had torn through the flesh in a perfect arc. The wound was deep and the blade had slid clear through to the windpipe, which explained why the mule's scream had been cut off so abruptly. But that was not all Davey saw.

On the bottom side of the neck the blade had struck the bone of the spine and broken off. He fished inside the wound with his index finger and retrieved the tip of the knife. He wiped the blood from it, revealing a black shiny material that he recognized at once. The blade had been made of obsidian and was perfectly chipped. He touched the tip and felt its sharpness, then ran his finger along the blade. The edge was keen as a honed razor.

There was that fluttering again in Davey's belly, and the hairs bristling on his neck and arms. He stuck the piece of blade in his possibles pouch and stood up. He knew who the mule belonged to now—it was Caleb Wakefield's—and he knew what had killed it. He wondered about the old trapper. There was no sign of him. It was odd, he thought, but he half expected that at any minute Caleb would walk up with his lean and angling gait and demand to know who had stolen his mule. That would have been the first thing the old man would do if his mule turned up missing—go and look for the animal.

But even as Davey waited there by the dead mule, he knew that Caleb wasn't coming. Not now, not ever.

With a heavy heart, Davey set out for the old trapper's digs, dreading what he would find there. The obsidian knife tip in his possibles pouch seemed to beat like a human heart and he could almost feel the heat of its glowing black blade searing his side.

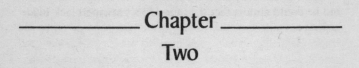

Chapter
Two

They came across the prairies from St. Louis when the snow was still on the ground, bringing their children, their animals, their tools, their bedding and mementos from another time. They came westward following crude maps, guided by the polestar and a westering instinct inherited from Nordic, Anglo-Saxon, and Teutonic ancestors. They followed the rivers and the migration trails of huge buffalo herds, marveling at such wide and surefooted roads.

They came in small groups and singly, traveling by night through tall prairie grasses, and sometimes they left shallow graves marked by wooden crosses or headstones pulled from the ground. They brought their musical instruments and churns, their froes and grandmothers' quilts and samplers. They carried their hopes with them, and their dreams. They carried files and pistols, and powder and lead, and flints and muslin and buckskins, a brick from the old chimney in Missouri or Tennessee, and jars of cookies and dried apples and apricots. They traveled by day under a bleak spring sun and forded swollen rivers at great peril, listening to their children scream in terror and their dogs bark at every prairie dog and prairie chicken that broke into startled flight as the wagon wheels creaked under the strain of loads that had to be lightened as the days wore on. They stopped to let the animals graze and spread blankets on the trampled grasses and held picnics under the shade of cottonwoods, and they drank from the rivers and felt the land swell under them and saw it stretch out to the distant horizon beyond the endless sea of grass. And then they saw the Rocky Mountains and came to the South Platte River and journeyed to places where the land was big and wide and the snowcapped peaks gave them a sense of wonder and awe they had never beheld before. There, they staked out their farms and broke out the plows and hauled their wagons into the foothills and brought down tall pines with axes and sawed them into cabin-wall lengths. They helped one another raise roofs and began to plow and plant. The women set up their stoves and hung their utensils on wooden pegs and made flapjacks and fried eggs and scrapple. The men butchered hogs and shot deer and quail and some went higher into the mountains and brought back elk meat and the women dried the meat and roasted shanks and shoulders on open fires at dusk, and the men bathed in the South Platte and came home hungry and tired and grateful that they still had potatoes and hot biscuits made from sourdough and gravy to wipe on tin and pewter plates when the meal was done.

The men tried to dig wells, but the ground was still frozen beneath the surface, so the women hauled water from the river and they made do. The families gathered at the river on Sunday mornings and prayed to God and thanked Him for giving them a president who bought this land from the French and gave them the land bearing his name—Jefferson Territory—and in their minds they saw towns and churches springing up and people coming from the East to settle and buy their goods and their crops and bring them fabrics and tools, and they sang old hymns and the men took turns preaching from the Bible and they each worshipped according to the customs of their forefathers and did not complain that they were all from different denominations and each had his own

idea of God. They prayed for good crops and rain, for health
and happiness, and when the services were over, they went
back to work. For they knew the summer would be short
and that they must prepare for a hard winter on the plains.
So they cut wood and stacked it in cords and read from the
Good Book at night before they went to bed, using the fad-
ing light of the evening so the coal oil for the lamps would
last until drummers finally showed up at that isolated place,
perhaps the following year or the year after that. And the
women made candles from tallow and cured the hides of the
animals killed for meat, and sewed rabbit skins together for
comforters, and when a buffalo was killed, they used their
hides for rugs and blankets that would keep them warm in
the winter.

But one family broke off from the other settlers and
headed for the South Platte River. They were loners by nature, taciturn, almost sullen, people said, but they were part
of the group of settlers who had journeyed from St. Louis to
that section of Jefferson Territory. This family was led there
by its patriarch, a man named Hans van de Groot. Over the
years Hans first dropped the *van* from his name, and then
the *de*, so that his name would seem more American. Hans
and his wife, Madeline, whom he called Maddy, and their
son, Kris, short for Kristian, and a girl named Sheila Stewart, who was their bondservant. There, where the Cache de
la Poudre flowed into the South Platte River, on a high knoll
overlooking the vast prairie to the south and east, Hans Groot
set out his stakes, taking acreage for each member of his
family. He very carefully marked out the site for his homestead and drove stakes and attached strings to them to lay
out the foundation for his house.

Hans and Kris plowed a furrow that marked the perime-
ter boundary of the land they claimed for their own and began to plow a field some distance from the place where they
planned to build their house. The two women, Maddy and

Sheila, pitched a tent and set up the cookstove, unloaded the wagon of foodstuff and cooking utensils, and began to make their home on the prairie, in the shadow of the Rocky Mountains.

It did not take long before the two women began to quarrel, as they always did. Maddy constantly scolded Sheila to be faster and Sheila, stubbornly, refused to move at all. Maddy railed at the girl, who was eighteen years old, a pretty, blue-eyed, blond-haired lass who wore a shapeless dress made of old flour sacks, cheap sandals, and a tattered straw hat. Maddy was a heavy-boned Dutch woman, with a thick neck, stout arms and legs, facial features that seemed made of hard dough, and long brown hair tied up usually in a bun. She wore a print skirt and a muslin blouse and a necklace made of mother-of-pearl, gold and silver rings on her fingers, a cameo brooch she had inherited from her Rotterdam-born mother.

"You I will beat before this day is over," Maddy said to Sheila. "Fetch the water from the river quick before too dark it gets. And firewood we will need and you must sweep the ground for the other tents and make sure there are no rocks."

"You give too many orders at once, Maddy. I can't do these things all at once and I can't remember which to do first."

"Just do them, you hear?"

"I will get the wood, then the water."

"No, the water you will fetch first, then the wood you will gather."

Sheila dreaded going to the river. The bank was slippery and the water raged from the melting snows high in the mountains. She would put it off as long as she could. It was hard enough getting wood for the fire. She had to cross the South Platte or venture up over the hill to the north and seek out the small groves of pine that were scattered here and there. She had heard wolves and coyotes at night, and there were always animal tracks. But the river was too swift and deep to cross and so she had to walk far to gather and cut wood, to places out of sight of the homestead.

Sheila quelled the dread in her heart and walked over to the dwindling woodpile to get one of the axes lying on a ramp of three short logs stacked there to keep the iron from touching the ground. Hans always kept his tools oiled and dry, out of the weather, when possible. Kris was responsible for the sharpening, except when he was working. Then Sheila had to use the file and whetstone to keep the edges keen.

"Where are you going?" Maddy asked sharply when Sheila neared the woodpile.

"I will fetch the wood first."

"I told you the water to get first."

"The wood gathering is the hardest task. Besides, I am afraid to go out there when it nears dark."

"You had better mind me."

"I will fetch the water when I get back," Sheila said stubbornly.

The fearsome Dutch woman stalked after the girl who was bound to her and was about to strike her when something flashed in the foothills. Sheila cowered to protect herself, but she, too, saw the splash of light beyond the river, somewhere above the lowest hills. Then there was another burst of light from farther away, to the south. The flashing continued for several seconds.

"What is that?" Maddy wondered aloud.

"I don't know," Sheila replied fearfully.

"The devil's work," Maddy decided.

Quickly, Sheila picked up one of the axes and stooped to snatch up the leather straps to tie the cut wood to her back. She ran toward the high knoll to the north before Maddy could stop her.

"You will pay for your disobedience," Maddy called after her, and then she was distracted as the closest light began to sparkle rapidly, as if replying to the southernmost flashes, and suddenly she felt as if someone was watching her, observing her every move.

A cloud passed over the sun a moment later, and Maddy felt a sudden chill as the lights flashed off and on in the foothills, queer lights that had no known source, but most certainly meant danger.

Maddy started walking toward the far field, where her husband and son were plowing ground for planting. Terrified, she wanted to scream at them to come and take her back to civilization, away from the strange flashes and the deserted homestead. She also wanted to slap Sheila's face for disobeying her and running off, leaving her all alone and at the mercy of demons.

Davey wondered why Caleb had come up this far. He had left his digs weeks ago to trap the lower ponds and prospect for gold on the South Platte, telling Davey that he would see him at the rendezvous on Cherry Creek. Perhaps Caleb was still down there, either trapping the ponds below the moraines or trying to pan gold in the rushing waters of the Poudre or the Platte. Perhaps one of his mules had gotten away and some poor starving Ute had killed it for food, meaning to come back for the meat later.

As he retraced the tracks of the mule and the Ute, Davey knew that he was only whistling in the wind. Caleb would not have let a good mule get away from him. He'd have tracked it to the ends of the earth. The old trapper was a stingy, possessive man, and he hated to lose even a penny.

No, something was very wrong, Davey knew. That dead mule wasn't killed for meat. That Ute meant to leave a message. A warning.

"A hell of a way to start a spring," he muttered as he ducked under a jutting tangle of squaw wood sprouting from under a pine branch. He studied the tracks more carefully, puzzled. The moccasin prints showed that the Ute had been following the mule through the forest, but there was something odd about them. Was the Ute deliberately herding the mule toward the corral or had he merely been following it?

At first glance, it seemed the mule was wandering on an aimless path, but as Davey rode alongside the two sets of tracks, he was struck by their pattern, so subtle he could not detect it at first, but after roaming back and forth over the trail as it changed course, he realized that the Ute was indeed herding the animal toward the shelter Davey had built. Not only that, but he found two or three places where the mule had stopped to rest before moving on. At such spots, the Ute's tracks had come very close to the mule's. A queasy feeling began in Davey's stomach. It was as though he could feel someone watching him, as though someone had been watching him all winter. He felt suddenly naked, imagining someone invisible to him standing or sitting not far away from his camp, watching him make the sets in the ponds, return to take out the dead beaver, and then carry the bodies to camp, where he skinned them out and stretched their pelts on willow withes. It unsettled him, but it was nothing like the sensation he had a few moments later when he saw a distinct change in the tracks.

At first Davey thought he'd misread the sign, but as he followed the tracks he realized that he hadn't. The Ute's tracks were in front of the mule's, indicating that he had been leading the animal away from wherever Caleb had holed up. So it wasn't a case of the mule running away from Caleb. The Ute had deliberately led the pack animal toward Davey's camp.

But why? Mules were valuable to any Plains Indian tribe and to deliberately steal one and then kill it seemed drastic and dramatic to Davey.

The tracks aged as Davey rode on, ducking under low-flaring spruce and pine branches and noticing the shattered remnants of juniper where bull elk had scraped the velvet

off the previous fall, the red core of their trunks looking like
bloody veins gored by the savage slicing of antler tips. He
crossed a talus ridge beneath a flat granite outcrop growing
out of a mountain, his horse's shod hooves ringing on the
flat gray stones, and descended into meadows and timber
downed by lightning, looking like graveyards or the decimated remnants of columns that once held up the roof of an
ancient Grecian temple, hushed places that seemed like
empty cathedrals with the tall pines forming a canopy under
the blue sky.

Davey began to try and reckon time, the time it took
the Ute to get the mule to Davey's camp, and he knew that it
had not been a short drive, but one of patient hours. He
watched the sun crawl across the sky and figured he had
been riding nearly two hours. The tracks filling up, blurring
in the soft places where grass, fed by the melted snows, was
pushing through and tiny flower buds nestled close to the
ground, almost invisible, little green egg-shaped bumps still
protected from the weather by the ungainly growth of new
trees and grasses.

The trail got more rugged and steep and admiration for
the determination of the Ute began to build in Davey's mind.
There were places where the mule seemed to have balked
and had to be pulled over deadfallen trees and around massive boulders. The Ute had known where Davey had his camp
and he had cut an unerring course for it through heavy timber
and tangled undergrowth, withered berry bushes where the
bears had fed the summer before, thickets of them clumped
on hillsides and in deep hollows between towering ridges.

How far did the Ute come? Davey asked himself as he
looked back at the snowcaps ringing him like fortress walls.
Was he to be led clear to the waters of the South Platte? Another half hour passed and the tracks led out of a small
clearing that rose up quickly after Davey topped a shallow
ridge dotted with stunted pine and burly spruce and gnarled

fir. He stopped his horse, looked long and hard at the empty place, and felt his skin crawl. Two horses lay dead at the fringe of the meadow, one a pinto, the other a bay mare he recognized as belonging to Caleb. Shivers coursed up his arms and his stomach roiled.

Still, Davey did not move. He stayed atop the ridge, peering in every direction. He waited long enough to assure himself that the horses were dead. They did not move and the faint breeze did not ruffle their manes.

Must have been a hell of a fight, Davey mused as his horse stood stock-still, snorting at the smell of death. Finally he rode down into the meadow, his finger just a breath away from the cocked trigger of his rifle. The dun gelding stepped carefully across the mushy ground. Patches of snow glistened in shady spots around the meadow; beyond, where the corpses of the horses lay, he saw only shadows, the trees thick, the silence deep.

Davey rode to his left, on the high side of the meadow, stopping every few steps to listen, to look down toward the lower part of the glade and to the place where he had first stopped. A jay hawked a string of invectives some distance away and he heard a crow call. In the sky, a lone buzzard circled, back from the summer climes of the south, wheeling slowly on the air currents, its path a scrawl of patient, invisible hieroglyphs.

Davey kicked the horse and it took a few more steps before stopping again at a gentle tug of the reins. Some sound, unidentifiable at first, scratched from somewhere beyond where the dead horse and mule lay.

Davey brought his rifle up to his chest, holding it at the ready. He hunched down in the saddle and listened.

Again the sound came, a low moaning that he could not decipher.

"Caleb?" he called.

There was no answer.

"Caleb, is that you?"

"Helllllp," someone cried, and Davey slipped from the saddle and stood next to his horse, listening carefully.

"Where are you?" he yelled, louder than before.

"Over here. That you, Davey?" This time Longworth recognized Caleb's voice and started walking toward the dead animals, using his horse for cover, matching its steps with his own.

"I'm coming, Caleb. Hold on."

"Quick, Davey. Come quick." The old trapper's voice was much clearer now. Closer.

Davey patted the horse's flank, urging it to step out faster. Davey broke into a lope, careful not to get too far ahead of his horse. He passed the carcasses of the dead animals and moved into the timber.

"Where are you Caleb?" he called, his voice pitched low.

"Over here, Davey. Godamighty, hurry, will you?"

Davey saw movement and his eyes tracked toward the motioning arm. Caleb Wakefield sat propped against a tree, his bearded face covered with blood. A patch of crimson and white glistened just above his forehead. Davey hurried over to the wounded man and tied his horse to a sprig pine.

He knelt down beside Caleb and looked at his face closely. He could see the pain in the old trapper's eyes.

"You got scalped," Davey said, wincing at the sight of the place where Caleb's topknot had been ripped from the skull.

"Sure enough, Davey, and shot, too. I got me a arrowhead in my side, too. Broke off the shaft back down the mountain. Feels big as a wooden stake in there."

"Maybe I can get it out," Davey said.

Caleb tried to laugh, but choked and spit up a gob of blood. "I—it's buried deep, hurts like hell when I move or talk."

"Then don't say anything while I go after it."

"No Davey, it's no use. I got something to tell you. And there ain't much time."

Caleb let out a long sigh and his eyes closed for a moment. It was then that Davey knew Caleb was dying. He would not see the sun set that day, and in the silence of the moment, Davey felt a wave of sadness sweep over him, something he had felt a long time ago, before he came into the mountains and left his grief behind in a valley somewhere in Ohio.

Chapter Four

Maddy kept running until she fell into her husband's arms. He swooped her up to keep her from falling or knocking him down.

"There, there," he said. "You are frightened, no?"

"What are all those lights up in the mountains?"

Kris came trotting up a moment later, panting for breath. He, too, was watching the flashing lights.

"I do not know," Hans said, "but I have seen soldiers do this with little tin mirrors."

"Yes, so have I," Kris said.

"Soldiers? Out here?" Maddy fought back the hysteria that threatened to overwhelm her. She felt like swooning, but she did not want to bring shame upon herself.

"It could be," Hans said.

"Why would soldiers be up in the mountains?" Kris asked. He was not stupid, but he looked like some lumbering oaf, his legs having outgrown his pants, leaving the cuffs dangling six inches above his ankles, a shock of unruly blond hair, and eyes set too close together straddling his pudgy nose. He and his mother could have been twins born years apart, so closely did they resemble each other. Hans was a barrel-chested, thick-necked stack of a man, with sturdy, ham-thick legs, an even larger nose than his son's, veined with scarlet threads coursing through wide pores, a liverish set of lips fat as grub worms and often browned and wet from the tobacco he chewed, cut from a gnarled twist he kept in his pocket.

Maddy's breathing settled into a regular rhythm as the hysteria dwindled away. "That Sheila, damn her," she said. "Ran away from me."

"You must punish her, Maddy," Hans told his wife, releasing his firm hold on her.

"Oh, I will give her a beating she will not soon forget," Maddy said.

"She is very disobedient," Kris said.

"She will learn to behave," his mother concluded. She looked again to the mountains, but she did not see the lights. She sighed. "They have stopped."

"Yes." Hans nodded. "We will walk you back to the camp, eh? I want to make some forms for the bricks. Tomorrow, you and Sheila can get mud from the river and begin to make the bricks for our home. Where did she run off to, eh?"

"She went to fetch wood," Maddy replied. "But I wanted her to do some other things first."

"You take that quirt to her and she will begin to mind you."

"The ungrateful wench," Maddy said, and Kris nodded dumbly, unable to find the words to support his mother's contempt for their bondservant.

Hans smiled. He liked to see his wife angry. He liked to see the fire in her eyes; it made for good loving when the lamps were snuffed in the darkness of night. He, too, looked up again to the mountains, but he could see no blinking of lights, and as far as he was concerned, whoever had been doing it was far away and of no matter on this fine day. The women would be busy making the bricks from rammed earth and soon the house would go up and they would no longer have to sleep on the cold hard ground.

* * *

Sheila stopped to rest on the east bank of the South
Platte where she had been gathering driftwood. Her thoughts
still swirled from her narrow escape from a certain beating
at the hands of Maddy. She might still catch it when she returned with the firewood, but for the moment she was safe.

The beatings had become more frequent since they left
St. Louis. It was as if the Groots, having left civilization behind, had become savages. Sheila did not understand why
the family she was bound to had become so cruel, so heartless. Every time she thought of her real mother, she began to
cry. The longing in her heart had not diminished, although
she had not seen her mother in six long years.

She had been twelve when Lorna Stewart sold her into
bondage. Sheila's mother had told her that she could no
longer care for her and that the Groots would take good care
of her, give her food and shelter, buy her clothing that Lorna
could not afford to provide. It was true, Sheila knew. Her
mother had worked as a washerwoman in Philadelphia, had
scavenged for food in the garbage of restaurants and fine
homes. Sheila had learned to do the same, fighting down the
revulsion she felt at eating scraps she'd had to obtain before
the roving bands of dogs got to them.

Sometimes she and her mother were reduced to beg-
ging on the streets. They were often chased away and hu-
miliated by constables. Few people took pity on them, but
taunted them from street corners, hurling invectives at them
as if they were less than human. Often Sheila would hear
her mother crying at night, when it was dark and they were
sleeping in some alley or behind a livery stable.

"Why are you crying, Mother?" she would ask.

"I'm crying for my dead husband and for the life we
have to live. I wish Duncan were still alive. I miss him so."

"I miss Daddy, too," Sheila would say, and then she

and her mother would weep together until they fell asleep in each other's arms.

The dawn was always cruel during those hard times. She remembered walking along Front Street, a burlap sack in hand, searching for scraps, thrown-away fish from the Mississippi, remembered, too, the stares and rude comments of sailors and stevedores, the gulls wheeling in the sky overhead, screeching for those same scraps. And the smells of the St. Louis waterfront, fishy, stale, the gusts from the dry sandhills meeting with the air over the dank water, the hoots of steam whistles and the chug of engines, the stench of dog droppings and whale oil, the smoke from stacks stretching out like dark scrawls against the pale morning sky.

She would look longingly at the fresh fish on the vendors' slabs, the produce from the nearby farms and small gardens, so green and enticing it made her mouth water, and sometimes she would try to steal some fruit, a peach or a plum or persimmon, but she was usually caught and chased away.

She learned in those years that there was no pity in the world, and her life with the Groots only reinforced those feelings. They treated their horses and mules and cows better than they treated her, she thought bitterly, wondering how many more of their beatings she could endure.

As the spring sun warmed her Sheila recalled the terrible winter. Hans had been determined to leave St. Louis in late December, and had convinced other settlers that they had a long way to go and would lose a year's crops if they did not arrive in Jefferson Territory in the spring. Sheila thought they were all crazy, and there were times when she thought none of them would be alive in the spring.

The wagons, drawn by horses and oxen, crossed frozen creeks and rivers, following a bewildering course they traced from crude maps. Huge herds of buffalo sometimes blocked their way and once two people were killed when their wagon overturned at the fording place on the Missouri, another when they crossed the Platte, and a child when they forded the North Platte.

They had seen Indians at Grand Island, and given them a wide berth, but she still remembered the smoke from their campfires and the steam rising from tepees, wanting to go inside and get warm when she was shivering from the cold and her feet were numb from walking in deep snow, and Maddy was beating her to keep up and to fetch firewood and water at every camp while she and her family stood by the fire rubbing their cold hands over the jumping flames.

Sheila thought there was no end to the prairie, to the high plains they trekked through Nebraska land, and when she saw the first buttes, she thought they looked old and mysterious and might provide shelter from the shrieking winds, the blowing snow, and the bitter cold. But the wagon train kept moving, making fewer miles each day, and the snows got deeper, the game more scarce, and the shelters fewer and far between.

There were always the rivers, however, the pathways to the new lands, and she had to break the ice into chunks with an ax and carry the chunks back to camp so that it could be melted for drinking water and for cooking. The Groots never came to her aid, but beat her and railed at her for her slowness, when it was all she could do to breathe the sharp air that burned her lungs and move her nearly frozen feet through drifts of snow that sometimes seemed warm when the numbness set in.

Sheila wondered what her mother would look like now if she could see her. Would she recognize me? she asked herself. Is she looking for me? Does she wonder where I am? It seemed to her that she had been taken away from her mother's world and she longed for St. Louis. She wanted to roam the streets looking for her mother and she conjured up pictures in her mind of finally finding her mother and embracing her, crying on her shoulder.

Sheila shook off the thoughts that always came to her when she was alone and was able to reflect on the past. She scooted away from the bank and stood up. There was still more wood to gather and the sun was falling away in the sky. Soon, she knew, it would be dark and she would have some moments to herself before she fell asleep.

A sudden thrill raced down her spine and her stomach fluttered in anticipation. Somehow, she knew, her life would change in this new land. Someone would come along and realize her plight and rescue her, take her back to St. Louis, reunite her with her mother. Who would it be? And when? She sighed deeply and searched for wood, letting her mind empty of thoughts that only tortured her. Nobody would come. She would never see her mother again. She was a prisoner of the Groots and they all hated her.

Sheila looked up at the sky, then at the range of mountains beyond the South Platte River. The mountains seemed so grand and distant and heartless. Empty of all hope, silent, immutable guardians of the land. Despite her resolve, as she picked up the last scraps of firewood, she began to weep. She felt as if the mountains were crushing her, weighing her down when she wanted to fly back to her true home. But even the memories of St. Louis were growing dim and it was often hard to picture her mother's face. Too often the visage was blurred and dark and she remembered now that she had seldom seen her mother smile. And that rare smile was already gone from memory, beyond her grasp. But she could still remember her mother's sobs, and with a sudden start, she realized the weeping sounded exactly like her own, desperate, hopeless, lost. The tears of someone abandoned by God and men, left to suffer in a cruel, heartless world.

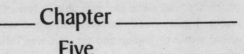

Davey knew that Caleb was dying. He could hear the rattle of impending death in the old trapper's throat and see the pain glazing his eyes like a thin winter frost. Catching Davey's long look, Caleb drew in a breath and his eyes sparkled for a brief moment.

"They's some life left in me, Davey. Don't start sayin' no prayers over me yet."

"I'm not, Caleb. What the hell happened anyway?"

"A pair of Utes jumped me down on the South Platte. I seen 'em watchin' me all the way down the mountain."

"You do anything to rile 'em up?"

Caleb paused as if gathering strength to go on. A tic struggled with a muscle in his cheek and caused his left eye to blink. It gave him an odd look, as if each of his eyes was moving independently of the other in their sockets.

"Didn't bother me none till I started panning in the river. I was just hunkered down by the bank, seein' what was bein' washed down by the Poudre. I was aswirlin' black sand and muddy water in my pan and these two bucks come up and signed for me to go away. They acted like they wanted me to give 'em my pan."

"What did you do?" Davey asked.

"I told 'em to go to hell."

"There's some reason they left you alive, Caleb. They could have cut your throat."

Caleb blinked his rheumy eyes, struggled for breath. A trickle of blood leaked from the corner of his mouth.

"I thought some about that," Caleb said. "Them two Utes chased me clear back up here. They could have killed me without running out of breath. Ever' time I tried to go back down, they cut me off. Then, when I got up here, they moved in and started chunkin' arrers at my hide. Then one of 'em scalped me real slick. He could have brained me with his war club, but he didn't."

"Did they tell you why they did this to you?" Davey asked.

Puzzlement flickered in Caleb's eyes as he squinted. "They made some signs I didn't reckon too good and the best I could make of it was they wanted me off the South Platte and didn't want me pannin' no gold."

Davey thought about Caleb's story. The Utes had never bothered the trappers before. In fact, they had traded some back when he had first come into the mountains. But they were a wary people. He had never felt trusted by them. He had noticed that they made their camps away from water, unlike the Arapaho, who camped along the Moonshell, what they called the South Platte River. The Utes stayed out of earshot of running water so that they could hear any enemy approach.

This was the first time Davey had heard that the tribe did not want white men to pan for gold in the South Platte. Not that there was any gold there that he knew of, but there could be, of course. He was not a prospector. The ones he knew who dug and panned for gold were strange, as if gripped by an unexplainable fever. He'd seen men fight over gold, seen men kill for it, and it was not a thing he wished to have or to seek.

"What signs did you not understand, Caleb?"

"Well, I understood 'em all right, but couldn't make no meaning outen 'em when I put 'em together."

"Like what?"

"Like 'mother,' 'father,' 'Great Spirit.' Maybe 'holy,' you know."

"No, I don't," Davey said.

"Something about the water in the South Platte bein' sacred, I guess."

"So you did understand what they meant," Davey said.

"Well, it didn't make no sense to me. I made the sign to drink and swim, and they didn't like it none. They did mention the shining metal, so I guess there must be gold in the Platte."

"Did you find any?"

"Didn't hardly have no time to look. Them red devils pestered me so damned much."

Davey said nothing. If the Utes held the South Platte sacred, then there could be trouble with the prospectors working on Cherry Creek, and soon the Cache de la Poudre. He had seen some gold seekers on Cherry Creek in the fall. They were a secretive bunch and he had not asked where they were panning.

"I should have stuck to trappin'," Caleb began again, leaning back against the tree to save his strength. "I sure did make a big mistake."

"Anything I can do for you?"

"You have any whiskey, Davey?"

"You know I don't."

"Well, I'd like to sleep through this, if I could."

"Through what? The pain?"

"No, the dyin'."

"I could maybe dig for that arrow tip."

"God, no, Davey. You wouldn't want to hear me hollerin'."

"If it would help, I could stand it."

Caleb tried to laugh, but he choked on blood and coughed a knot of it from his mouth, spraying rosy specks onto Davey's sleeve.

"Maybe you better just rest and ride it out, Caleb."

"Oh, they left me some life to chaw on, I reckon. Wanted me to think about what I done."

"I don't think that's why they didn't kill you right off, Caleb."

"No? What other reason?"

"I think they wanted you to tell me why they shot you and scalped you."

"That don't make no sense, Davey."

"Not right off, maybe. But those same two Utes could have killed me, too."

"Not you, Davey. You got Injun ways. Them Utes know it. You could smell 'em comin'."

"Look, Caleb, one of 'em run your mule right up in my corral and then killed him there. He wanted me to backtrack him and find you."

"That don't make no sense neither."

"It does if the Utes want me to be a messenger for them."

"A messenger?"

"Looks like they don't want any white men trampin' around their territory."

"Hell, they like our whiskey and beads well enough."

"Maybe not. Maybe not anymore."

Caleb snorted weakly. "You alluz could think like an Injun."

"No, Caleb. I just put myself in their place sometimes. I can see that the Utes might think there are too many of us coming into their country."

"Well, what are you going to do, Davey? Run off, leave all the beaver to 'em? The gold?"

"I haven't seen any gold. There's beaver other places."

"You're scared, Davey. You are going to run off."

"I don't know, Caleb. I'm sure as hell going to watch my backtrail real hard."

It was true. Davey didn't know what he was going to do. He wondered if he could pull Caleb through, pack his wounds with snow and mud and see if he could heal up enough to get back down the mountain. He looked at the man, as if assessing his chances, and Caleb returned his stare. There was sadness in his look and Davey felt a chill race up his spine, as if someone had just walked over the place where his grave would one day be.

"It ain't no use, Davey. I can feel my blood running inside, like a river going down a hole in the ground."

"There's always hope, Caleb," Davey said, but his heart was sinking like a stone in that same river Caleb spoke about.

_____ Chapter _____
Six

Hans Groot worked his family from dawn to dusk. He and his son, Kris, plowed the first field and planted it. When they finished work each day, they laid the dried brick the women had made the previous day. Slowly, the house began to rise on its foundation. It was being built like a small fort, with holes for gun ports and logs stacked against the inner walls for protection. At night, Sheila and Maddy dug a cellar by candlelight. The men brought the tents inside and they slept behind the rising walls.

Sheila wondered what drove such people to work so hard. She could not stop until Maddy did and often they worked past the midnight hour, shoveling dirt and carrying it outside, down steps the men had built, stumbling through the dark. The dirt was used the next day to make more rammed-earth bricks and the work went on, with fatigue replacing physical cruelty in Sheila's life. She felt as if she was gaining a second wind as the welts on her back and legs and arms gradually healed and the sun tanned her fair skin.

But the long hours and the lack of sleep sapped her strength, so that it was hard to get up in the mornings when Maddy called to her. One morning, after a long night of digging out the basement, Sheila lay in the lean-to outside of the cabin, unable to rise. Maddy had called her several times and she had answered, "I'm coming," but she could not will herself to climb out from under her thin blanket.

"She does not come," Hans said as he swirled a slab of scrapple through a pool of sorghum.

"Sheila, come here right this minute," Maddy called again.

Kris chewed on a piece of tough scrapple and blinked his eyes. "She does not answer this time," he said. "Do you want me to go and get her?"

Maddy and Hans exchanged glances. Lately their son had shown a new interest in Sheila and they had talked about it. Maddy had noticed Kris staring at the bondservant when he thought no one was looking. She had said nothing to Kris, but to her husband she remarked about it more than once. "He needs a girl to court, not that worthless wench," was Maddy's opinion.

"No, it is not good he has the eyes for Sheila," Hans had told her. "I will speak to the boy."

But Hans had not spoken, and Kris's infatuation with Sheila threatened to get out of hand.

Hans looked at Maddy and shrugged.

"Bring her," Maddy said, "but be quick about it."

"Yes, Mama."

Sheila lay in a numb stupor; the voices in the big room seemed far away, outside of time. She felt as if she were floating somewhere outside instead of sleeping under a lean-to. The morning cold did not penetrate her thin blanket, nor did the cold ground gnaw at her as it usually did. She looked at her sore hands in the pale morning light. They seemed to be the hands of a fifty-year-old woman, not her hands at all. They were begrimed with dirt that would not wash out in the river's cold water, but only darkened each day.

Tears began to stream down her face as she lay there, almost beyond feeling, except for the emptiness inside her that was like a thundercloud, as if she had been sapped of life. Robbed of love and tenderness and kicked outside the stream of living people.

She heard the pad of footsteps across the boards that had been laid down over the hollowed-out earth of the basement. The voices faded away and she could distinguish only the faint scratching of a fork across a pewter plate. Then she heard the heavy thud of footfalls on the steps outside the house.

Sheila drew her hands back inside the blanket and curled herself into a ball, pulling her knees up to her chest and wrapping her arms around her legs. She closed her eyes and waited for Maddy to kick her under the lean-to. She listened to the dull pound of feet on the ground as someone walked around the house and toward her lean-to, on the western side where the sun had not yet struck.

The footfalls stopped beside Sheila's lean-to, and she braced herself for a kick from Maddy. Instead, she felt a hand on her thigh. Puzzled, she froze, her eyes closed. Then a hand grabbed her breast. She twisted away, her eyes wide. Then the hand on her thigh moved up between her legs, and the hand on her breast shifted to her mouth, clamping it tightly shut.

"Pretty girl," a voice rasped.

Sheila stared into the face of Kris as he slid down beside her. She clamped her legs together on the hand probing her privates. A finger poked at her panties and she cringed in terror.

"Mmmf," was all she could utter as Kris's hand pressed against her lips, hurting her. She squirmed and wriggled her lower body to dislodge the young man's other hand. "Stop," she said, but the word was muffled by the pressure on her mouth.

"Be quiet, Sheila," Kris whispered. "I ain't going to hurt you."

Sheila lifted her hands and grabbed Kris by his wrist;

she pulled desperately at the hand pressing down on her mouth. It came free and she screamed.

"Damn you," Kris said, and removed his hand from between her legs.

"Get away from me, Kris, or I'll kick you." Sheila brought her knees up to deliver a blow to Kris's groin and he stood up, his face reddening from shame. She kicked at him and one foot struck his right shin.

"Ow," he cried, and staggered backward.

"You filthy animal," she cried, and then began to scream even louder than before.

Kris snarled at Sheila. "You better not say nothing about this, you little bitch."

"Go to the devil, Kris," Sheila spat. She could still feel the heat of his hand on her breast, the attempted violation between her legs. She wanted to pick up something and throw it at him.

"What is going on here?" they heard Maddy ask as she rounded the corner of the dwelling.

"I woke her up," Kris said. "She tried to kick me."

A half second later Hans hove into view, puffing with exertion, clots of syrup lodged in the corners of his mouth.

"You kicked my son?" Maddy screamed, storming toward Sheila, who was just then crawling out of her lean-to. "How dare you?"

"Papa, that girl's no good," Kris said, avoiding his father's eyes. "I hate her."

"Go on inside the house," Hans ordered.

"Yes, Papa," Kris said, his face still flushed from shame and humiliation, and disappeared around the corner of the house.

Maddy slapped Sheila as the girl rose to her feet. Sheila, her face a composite of hurt and surprise, brought a hand up to touch the place where she was struck. She backed away, nearly stumbling over a tent stake.

"I'll teach you to strike our son," Maddy screamed.

"Don't you hit me, Maddy. Your son tried to . . . to do something to me."

"What?" Maddy caught herself up short, the hand she held high suddenly frozen.

"You heard me. Kris had his hands all over me, on my privates."

"You are a liar," Hans said, his voice booming in the silence.

"I'm not lying," Sheila insisted, still backing away.

"You shut your mouth, or I will shut it for you," Hans warned.

"Are you going to let her get away with this, Hans?" Maddy asked. "She should be beaten to within an inch of her life."

"She will be punished." Hans's voice was low and menacing.

"You hear that, you little tramp," Maddy screeched. "You will be punished."

"It is Kris who should be punished," Sheila said, her face still stinging from Maddy's blow.

"You shut your mouth and keep it shut," Maddy told her, advancing on her again.

Sheila did not back away. "Go ahead and hit me again. It won't change the truth," she said. "Kris touched me on my privates and tried to get into my bed."

Maddy started to say something, but Hans stopped her. "This is not the time," he said. "I will take care of this."

"Are you going to let her lie about our boy?" Maddy asked.

"It is time to get to work. I will handle this later. Go back into the house and I will send the girl to fetch water."

"She needs a beating," Maddy said sourly. But a look from Hans sent her sheepishly back to the half-finished structure.

Hans stared at Sheila, and she glared at him.

"I do not want more trouble from you."

"Ask your son what he did," Sheila said stubbornly.

"It does not make any difference what Kris did. You are a temptress and I will not have you seducing my son. Do you understand?"

"Mr. Groot," Sheila said slowly, "I hate your son. He is the last person I would want in my bed."

"Be careful you do not say too much, Sheila. I am doing all I can now not to break your neck. Now, get the buckets and fetch the water from the river. By the time you get back, Kris and I will be out in the field."

With that, he turned away and walked slowly around the corner of the house. He did not look back.

Sheila watched him go, the anger in her blazing white-hot. She knew now that the whole family hated her and none would take her side. At that moment she realized she could no longer stay with the Groots. She could no longer endure such treatment. And now she was fearful for her life. She had no doubt Hans had meant what he said. Someday, if his temper flared, he would take those big hands of his and break her neck.

Sheila shivered at the thought.

Chapter
Seven

Davey listened to Caleb's labored breathing for several moments. He wondered how long the old trapper could last.

As if reading Davey's thoughts, Caleb looked up into the sky. "Ain't no buzzards circlin'. Like as not I ain't done yet."

"I better go in after that arrowhead, Caleb."

"Just let me be, Davey. A man has the right to die if'n he wants to, don't he? And if he can, the way he wants to."

"It ain't right to make me suffer along with you, Caleb. I got better things to do."

"Just you go on, then. But before you go, I got somethin' to tell you."

"I'm listening," Davey said.

"I cached my furs, Davey. You know the place."

"Yeah, Caleb, I know the place."

"Other cache is on this side of the Platte."

"Not the other side?"

"Nope, I seen homesteaders on the other side and I didn't want 'em takin' my pelfries."

"Homesteaders?"

"Couldn't make 'em out none too well, but they warn't there last summer when we come up."

"Maybe that's what got the Utes stirred up."

"Don't know, but they're aplowin' and abuildin'. Saw me a couple of wimmen and a couple of men. One gal was young, I reckon, with hair as gold as a sunflower."

"Damn," Davey said.

"Anyways, that cache is marked with my blaze. You take twenty paces north and you'll see a pair of rocks stacked like. Then you pace out a dozen steps west and it's under some deadfall and brush. I want you to have what I cotched."

"Christ, Caleb, I don't want your damned pelts. You let me at that arrowhead and get 'em yourself."

"Hell, if I let you at me with your knife, even if you dug out that black chunk, I'd be weeks gettin' to where I could walk, and that'd be slow as a sick snail."

"Life is better than death, Caleb."

"I had me a good 'un."

Davey didn't know what to say. Caleb had made up his mind to die, and there was a good chance he couldn't be saved anyway. He was filling up with his own blood and his eyes were more glazed than before. The man had to be feeling a lot of pain, too. He wished he had some whiskey to give him, but he had none, and no medicines for what Caleb had.

"You want a drink of water?" Davey asked.

"Couldn't keep none of it down."

The two men were silent for several moments. Caleb was struggling to breathe, hawking up blood and phlegm every few seconds. His chest sounded as if it was full of fluid; there was a steady rasp to his every breath now.

"Help me sit up more," he managed finally.

"Sure," Davey said. He pulled Caleb up against the tree. He could feel the old trapper wince as he let him down gently.

"I'd like to see a Rocky Mountain sunset one more time, Davey."

"Well, you might. I just hate sittin' here watching you struggle."

"You can go anytime you want. I ain't afraid."

"Nothin' much to be afraid of now," Davey said.

"Nope, not a thing."

Caleb went into another coughing fit and sprayed blood all over the ground. Tiny red flecks spattered the pine needles and winter-browned aspen leaves. Davey held his shoulders until the fit had passed. Now Caleb was trembling, as if the effort to stay alive had sapped him of his remaining strength. Davey had seen a horse tremble like that after being run to a lather. The horse foundered and died.

Davey looked away and thought about what Caleb had said about seeing another sunset before he died. Some evenings during the winter, he had sat outside his shelter watching the sky turn to fire, the clouds all molten and bronzed by the setting sun, and sometimes they were the color of salmon, pink like the flesh of a trout, and he would watch the sky turn purple over the high frozen peaks and feel the night close around him, and it was a good feeling at the end of a hard day wading through the beaver ponds, the water so cold it froze his mind, and he knew it had been a good day and he would sleep peaceful through the bitterly cold night.

Caleb coughed, a weak, watery cough that forced blood from his mouth. He twitched as he sat up straighter and Davey knew the old mountain man was feeling the arrow tip inside him gouge into his flesh. Then Caleb started to fall over. Davey reached for him and propped him back up. The old man wiped fresh blood from his lips.

"I ain't afeerd of dyin', Davey. I done it many times before," he assured him.

Davey looked surprised. "Oh, yeah?"

" 'Bout six times, I figger. Come close, anyways. So, I done worked it out in my mind, a long time ago."

"And what did you decide?" Davey asked.

"Well, I figger I'll come back as somethin' else next time. A buffler, maybe, or an antelope. Or maybe a homely old buzzard. I figger I can pick what I come back as."

"Could be," Davey said, with a wry smile breaking over his face. "I've heard such before."

"Preacher says man got him a soul and Injuns figger everything on earth has a soul. Only they call it spirit. They take a lot of stock in that. So I don't figger to come back as a man, but as some animal or a plant maybe."

"A hell of a thing," Davey said, puzzled at such talk. But Caleb was dying and a dying man was liable to say anything. Maybe he was losing his mind from spilling so much blood. Addled, maybe.

"Don't make no difference nohow, I reckon."

Davey didn't say anything. Let old Caleb ramble on, if he wanted to.

"If you die and it all goes black, then you got no worry. You're dead and gone forever. If you got a soul, maybe that soul goes somewhere, eh? Maybe to a better place. Maybe out there in the stars, like the Injuns say."

"And what's out there in the stars, Caleb?"

Caleb laughed and something inside him seemed to tear loose, because he doubled up in a paroxysm of coughing and splattered blood.

Davey grabbed him as he fell forward away from the tree, and he heard the trapper gasp for breath. Caleb gave a great shudder and Davey felt him go limp in his arms.

"Caleb?"

There was no answer. Davey propped the trapper up and saw that his eyes were closed, shut tight as if he had gone into the darkness afraid, after all.

Davey cocked his head and put his ear close to Caleb's mouth. He listened, but could not hear the old mountain man breathing. "Caleb?" he called again, but he knew the old man was gone. He waited a few minutes to see if Caleb would come back to life, but the trapper's body grew heavy and his chest was not moving.

"Good-bye, old friend," Davey whispered, and choked back tears. "I hope you find a place in the stars."

Then he sat back and let Caleb's body slump forward. He would pack him back to camp and bury him there, put some stones over him to keep the wolves from eating him right away. Then he would finish packing and go down the Poudre and leave his cache before going on to Cherry Creek to meet the trader from Bent's Fort. It was time to leave the mountains, time to get on with his own life and forget about death, and about the Ute who led him to this place to watch his friend die.

"I'll be seeing you, Caleb," Davey said as he rose to his feet, and he thought he heard an echo of the trapper's voice whispering through the pines. But it was only a gust of spring breeze come down from the high peaks to breathe new life into the living.

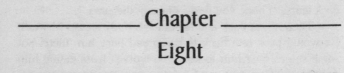

Chapter Eight

Gauzy morning mist hung over the Cache de la Poudre River and flowed into the South Platte, where it thickened into a heavy brume. Davey Longworth had mixed feelings about fog. He liked the comfort it gave him when he was riding through Indian country, the cloak of invisibility. But he didn't like riding blind, unable to see far ahead of him, behind him, or anywhere else.

He rode now inside the fog, the ground dropping away from him and the pair of mules laden with furs following behind. The horse was skittery and he didn't know if it was from the fog or something the animal could smell and didn't like much. He had found Caleb's caches, and made his own, working in the half dark so that he would have less chance of being seen and having his furs unearthed and stolen. He'd had a good winter of trapping, marred only by Caleb's death and a few minor mishaps with frozen traps, wolves that robbed him of a few beaver, and a twisted ankle that he blamed on his own carelessness.

Davey forded the Platte above the place where the Poudre joined it. The water was not so swift there, and not as deep. The horse swam well, seemingly eager to get to the other side, and the mules followed blindly, reassured perhaps by the steady tug on the lead rope.

His horse and the mules shook off the water when they gained the high ground on the opposite shore of the South Platte and Davey dismounted to check the panniers laden with furs, grub, bedroll, blankets, and cooking utensils. The diamond hitches had held, although the wetness stretched the ropes some. He wondered if his powder was dry in the horn, the air was so wet, the fog so thick he could not see ten feet ahead of him.

He had observed no sign of Utes on his ride down the Poudre, no sign that any were following him or marking his progress. The stillness, especially when he crossed the moraines, had been eerie. Not even a birdcall or the early whistle of a young elk. It was as if the world was dead and he was the only one alive. Spooky.

He had made camp the night before a few miles upriver and had listened intently into the evening for any footfall or crackle of rock, but there was only the shroud of the night and the walls of mountains, silent as mute sentinels, rising above him, and the soft susurration of the breezes through the lofty pines. He had made no fire and slept away from the false camp, just to be on the safe side. Some fur bales under a blanket out in the open, and he holed up in a copse of spruce several yards away, partially submerged in an old mule-deer wallow.

His horse shied at something and pranced off the trail, sidling stiff-legged, his ears perked to bristling cones.

"What is it, boy?" Davey whispered, and the dun gelding balked for a moment until Davey ticked his flanks with his heels. Then his mount straightened up and he reined him back onto the trail. The trail was like the one he had followed across the plains, a wide swath of trampled earth made by huge herds of buffalo over centuries of winter-spring migrations. This one was an old game trail, but was still used by the Utes and Arapaho during the same seasons. All of these trails had become like highways to Davey and many a traveler on the frontier.

As his horse neared the confluence of the Poudre and the South Platte, Davey heard splashing and the dun pricked up its ears again.

Davey rode close to the river. Along the shore the mist was stirring, breaking up into swirling wisps and giving him better visibility. Ahead, he saw a figure struggling against the slippery bank, sliding backward, gaining a foot or two, and then skidding down toward the water.

"Need any help?" he called as he swung down from his horse.

"What?" The voice was lyrical sounding, and the moment he heard it Davey knew that it belonged to a woman.

"You look as if you're in need of help." He stepped closer and saw a golden-haired girl, a woman, really, trying to negotiate the steep bank with two large wooden buckets in her hands. The buckets were sloshing water over the sides, making the bank even more slippery.

"I can manage," the woman said.

"No trouble. Just hand me your buckets and I'll help you get up that bank."

"I don't need your help, mister. Best you ride on and mind your own business."

"It's not every day a man gets to play Good Samaritan," Davey quipped.

"Best you go on."

"Nonsense." He stepped close, reached out a hand. "Give me one of the buckets at least."

Reluctantly, the woman handed him one of the buckets. He set it down and reached for the other one. The woman hesitated, then swung her arm upward. Davey grabbed the rope handle of the bucket and set it down beside the first.

"Name's Davey Longworth," he said. "Give me your hand and I'll pull you up. No use your slipping back down that muddy bank."

"Oh. Well, I guess so." She stretched out her hand and

Davey clasped it, drew her toward him. She was light as a feather, pretty as any woman he'd ever seen. She had startling blue eyes and that sun-gold hair set her apart. Her cheeks glowed with a pink hue in the fog-soft light.

"And your name?" Davey asked.

Breathless, the woman put a hand on her chest as if to gather her wits about her. She pushed aside a wisp of hair that caressed one cheek.

"I—I'm Sheila," she said. "Sheila Stewart. I mean Groot."

"Well, which is it?" Davey asked, smiling. "Groot or Stewart? Are you married?"

"Why, no—I'm not married, it's just that . . ." She smoothed her dress with both hands, shifted her feet as if she were uncomfortable.

"Divorced?" Davey offered.

"I'm bound to the Groot family," Sheila said.

"A bondservant?"

She nodded.

"Well, that's nothing to be ashamed of," Davey said. "How long have you been with the family?"

"Six years, I think. Yes, six years."

"Six years? That's a long time."

"Yes." Sheila frowned. "Now I must go, really."

"I'll help you carry the water up. Where to?"

"No, no," she protested. "You mustn't."

"But I want to meet the people you work for," Davey said. He bent over to pick up the buckets. As he stretched out his arms he heard the snap of a rifle lock. A chill stretched along his spine like an icy finger and he froze.

Davey waited for the explosion from the rifle. Then he felt the cold iron of the muzzle press against his neck. He drew in a breath and waited for the click of the trigger being squeezed. It seemed to him that his heart stopped dead in that long agonizing moment.

Chapter Nine

The instant the cold steel of the rifle barrel pressed against his neck, Davey Longworth knew that he would not let his life be taken so easily.

"Mister, let me stand up," he said. "If you're going to shoot me, at least look me in the eye when you do it."

"You stand up. Move slow and turn around." The voice was gruff, with an accent that sounded somehow familiar. He rose up slowly and turned around, his hands over his head. Before him stood a stocky, florid-faced man with a neck as thick as a nail keg. He had a fleshy button nose and close-set blue eyes that were pale as robins' eggs. Like Sheila, he wore a coat over a sweater to ward off the morning chill.

Davey and Sheila exchanged glances. Davey saw a look in her eyes that he hadn't noticed before. It made him feel uncomfortable, for it was as if she was viewing him as her savior, someone who would take her away, be her champion. But there was more behind the look than that, and he was surprised, since he felt drawn to her, not out of pity, but from some other emotion that had lain dormant for years.

Davey broke the connection between them, but he wondered if Groot had noticed the pleading in Sheila's eyes, the longing in his own brief gaze. He brought his attention back to the man he assumed to be one of the Groots.

"Are you going to shoot me?" Davey asked calmly.

"Just you go, mister. You keep your hands off my girl."

"Mr. Groot," Sheila started to say.

"Just you keep the mouth shut, Sheila," Groot said.

"Mister," Davey protested, "all I did was help this woman get those water buckets up on the bank. Now put that rifle away before one of us gets hurt."

"I put the rifle down," Groot said, "but you must leave this place."

"Not very friendly, are you?"

"We have few friends."

"In this country, you need every one you can get."

"We get by," Hans said. He looked suspiciously at Davey, but began to step backward. The rifle barrel wavered and sank slightly.

"You seen any Utes around here?" Davey asked.

"Utes? What is that?"

"Indians. They killed a friend of mine the other day."

"We do not see any Indians," Groot answered.

"That's the trouble, mister. You don't see them, but you can bet they have their eyes on you."

Hans looked around as if expecting to see an Indian spring up out of nowhere. That's when Davey jumped him, snatching the rifle from his hands.

"You—you tricked me," Hans sputtered.

"It's not very polite to put a gun on a man you don't know," Davey told him.

"Tell him about the lights, Mr. Groot," Sheila urged.

"What?" Hans looked dumbfounded.

"The flashing in the mountains," Sheila reminded him.

"You keep your mouth shut," Hans told her.

"But I . . ." Sheila started. A look from Hans made her close her mouth.

"What's this about lights?" Davey asked.

"It was just soldiers," Hans said. "They use the mirrors to make the messages. It was nothing."

"There are no soldiers this far north," Davey said. "Not this time of year. And if there were, they wouldn't be up in the mountains."

Hans's face flushed, turning his flesh a rosy paste color. "What do you mean? I have seen only soldiers use the mirrors to make the signals."

"The Indians use 'em, too. Mostly Utes. They can make sign a long way. Something's up, that's for sure. When they make talk like that, they're not just discussing the weather. I better take a look at your place, Groot. You could be in danger."

"We are not afraid."

Davey snorted in disgust. "Mister, do you know where you are?"

"Yes. We are on land we claimed. We are home."

Davey heaved a sigh, as if dealing with a child who was playing with fire and did not understand the danger. He hefted Groot's rifle, checked the lock, stock, and barrel. "How many of these do you have?" he asked.

"My son and I have two rifles and two pistols each."

"Well, you could maybe last two minutes, three at the most, if a swarm of Utes came down out of those hills and attacked you. And then there's the Arapaho. They claim this land, too."

"Arapaho?"

"Let's go up to your place. I'll explain on the way. Maybe I can help. See what kind of defenses you have, where your house sits."

"It's up on the hill there." Hans pointed. "You come, you look, then you go, eh?"

"I didn't plan to linger."

Davey screwed out the flint, stuck it in his pocket.

Then he gave the rifle back to Groot. "I'll give you back your flint when you calm down some," he told him.

"You tell me about these Arapaho," Hans said.

Davey stooped down and picked up the buckets. Hans frowned. Sheila tried to wrest them away from the trapper, but he shouldered her aside. "I'll carry these," he said to her. "You pull my horse and pack mules, okay?"

She nodded. Hans still wore a scowl on his face.

"She should carry the water," he insisted.

"It's no trouble," Davey said lightly. "Easier for her to pull the horse and mules. Water's heavy."

"That is her job," Hans insisted stubbornly.

Davey let it go. There was no use arguing with the man. He was obstinate and hardheaded. He had met his kind before.

The three walked up the gentle slope toward the Groot homestead. The fog was lifting, and as it thinned Davey saw the makings of the house on the center of the rise. At least, he thought, the man has a good view of the country on all sides. He had passed this place before. He never thought he'd see a soddy sitting on that comely hill, with the tall gamma and gramma grass cut away all around. He could smell the fresh earth from the plowed ground and it brought back memories of his own childhood in the East.

"This place where we're walking now," Davey said, "is a highway."

"A highway? What do you mean?"

"See how the ground is torn up, the grass short? Huge buffalo herds come through here, along the South Platte. The Utes, Arapahos, Cheyennes, are all dependent on those herds for food, shelter, and clothing."

"We see these buffalo trails when we come from St. Louis," Groot said.

"Where you built your home is right next to the path

the buffalo use. And the Indians think of the buffalo as almost like a god. It is their main food source and they make blankets and clothes from the hides, use the sinew for thread, the fat for soap, the bones for needles and fishhooks."

"We did not know," Hans said.

"Are there are no other settlers close by?" Davey asked.

"No. There are some to the east of us and to the south."

"You may have picked a bad spot to take up farming."

"It is a good spot," Hans said stubbornly.

"If the Arapaho and the Ute let you stay."

"I have thought of that," Hans said.

"Oh?"

"We have brought with us many trinkets. We hear the Indians like to trade these things. We also have coffee, tobacco, beads, thread. We will pay for the land if that is necessary."

Davey shook his head. He listened to the water sloshing in the buckets as they neared the partially completed structure at the top of the knoll. A young man and a woman stood outside. The man held a rifle in his hands and the woman held a hoe as if it were a weapon.

"If you want to trade with the Indians, if you want to make friends with them," Davey said, "I'd be careful about starting out a conversation with a rifle in your hands. Like you did with me."

"I thought you were going to harm Sheila. I was protecting what is mine."

Davey winced at Groot's choice of words. He looked back at Sheila, who was following behind them, and saw that her face was waxen, taut, as if she had been slapped. He was beginning to sense that she had strong emotions, resented being a bondservant. He wondered if Groot knew how she felt.

"Out here," Davey said, "there's some who would take a dislike to a man owning another person."

"Sheila is mine. I paid for her," Hans said.

Davcy frowned. "Oh? Then you must hold with slavery. There is a time limit on such servitude."

"I mean she is mine under bond until she has paid back the money I gave for her."

Davey was developing a strong dislike toward Hans Groot. Something inside him bucked at the idea of human bondage. In a free land such as this, he could not fathom a girl like Sheila working in servitude for a man like Groot.

But, at the same time, Davey told himself that it was none of his business.

Or was it?

Chapter
Ten

As Davey and the others came closer to the house, Hans called out, "Kris, put away the rifle. Maddy, bring some coffee. We have a visitor."

Maddy set down her hoe and turned toward the steps. Kris stood there for a long moment until his mother spoke to him, then he leaned the rifle against the side of the steps.

"My wife and son," Hans said to Davey.

"I welcome the taste of coffee. I ran out two or three weeks ago," Davey said.

"Papa, are you all right?" Kris asked.

"I am just fine, Kris. We have a stranger to visit us," Hans replied. His accent seemed even thicker now that he was with his family. Groot turned to Davey and said, "I do not know your name."

Davey told him, loud enough for Kris to hear. The young man did not nod or smile. Instead, he glanced at his rifle as if measuring the distance from him to it, the time it would take him to shoot.

"Give to Sheila the buckets," Hans said to Davey. "She must help my wife."

A few feet from the house, Davey set the buckets down. Sheila picked them up obediently and carried them up the steps and into the partially completed shelter. Davey retrieved the dangling reins and led his horse and the mules to the side of the house, where he looped the reins around a log that had not yet been set inside the dwelling. He noticed the tent alongside and figured that Sheila was the one who was made to sleep outside the safety of the walls.

All around the house were signs of activity. He noted the forms for the rammed-earth bricks, the pile of dirt, a pair of buckets still full of soil, hammers, saws, a keg of nails. Beyond, he saw the wagon and the shelter for the mules, and stacked firewood, a small cart.

Maddy brought out a tray with four tin cups and a steaming pot of coffee. She set the tray down on the top step. Hans handed Davey a cup. Kris and Maddy picked up cups. She gave her husband one and poured his coffee first.

"You are a trapper?" Maddy asked Davey.

"Yes'm. A free trapper."

"You do not work for a company?" Maddy said.

"No'm, I don't." Davey sipped the coffee. It tasted of cinnamon. "Good coffee, ma'am."

Maddy's lips curved in a thin smile. She sipped her own coffee and regarded the buckskin-clad stranger warily. Davey thought that she might even be sniffing him.

"You are passing through?" Maddy asked.

"I'll be taking my pelfries to Cherry Creek," Davey replied. When the woman looked puzzled, he pointed to the south. "Yonder," he said.

"You will sell the furs there?"

Davey told them about the trader who came out from Bent's Fort in the spring.

"There is much money in furs?" Hans asked.

"A man can do well by himself."

Davey wondered what Sheila was doing. It was obvious to him that the Groots did not consider her part of their family. Just a bondservant. He heard the clatter of pots and pans, the slosh of water from inside the shelter, sounds that the Groots did not seem to notice.

Reaching into his pocket, he fished out the flint he had taken from Hans, along with the scrap of leather used to hold it tight in the lock's vise. Hans took the items, but did not reattach them to his rifle. Kris looked at his father in puzzlement, but said nothing.

The four drank the rest of their coffee in silence. Davey could feel the air of suspicion that had seemingly sprung up around him. There was an almost palpable hostility connecting the stolid Groots to each other as they gazed at him over the rims of their tin cups.

"You've made a good start here," Davey commented, setting his cup down on the tray. "It would be a pity if you lost it all."

Hans bristled. "What do you mean?"

"The Utes are likely to go on the warpath one of these days and you'll probably have some Arapaho braves stop by to see what you're doing on their hunting grounds."

"We have as much right to live here as they do," Maddy said belligerently.

"That may be your point of view. This place is pretty special to a lot of tribes, even to the French and Spaniards. This is where the Cache de la Poudre runs into the South Platte, a kind of crossroads, you might say. In the summer, the Arapaho and the Southern Cheyenne follow the South Platte up from the south, from New Mexico, and they stop here. Some go up the Poudre to hunt for deer and elk. And all the tribes follow the buffalo. So you're right smack-dab in the middle of powerful medicine country. I think that's why the Utes killed my friend Caleb and took his scalp."

Maddy winced and Kris shifted his weight. Hans's neck swelled like a bull elk in the rut and his florid face blossomed to an even deeper roseate hue.

"Perhaps your friend did something to make the Utes mad," Hans suggested.

"He did," Davey admitted.

"What did he do?" Maddy asked.

"He panned for gold in the South Platte. The Utes consider the river a gift of the Great Spirit, sacred waters, so to speak."

"Well, we would never do that," Hans said. "We give to the land the seeds and we take what the seeds give to us. It is a different thing."

"Could be." Davey shrugged. "If you can explain that to the tribes hereabouts and they understand it, you may be all right."

"We plan to trade some of our crops to them," Hans said. "Barter."

"You could start by giving them some corn or wheat," Davey suggested. "Indians love gifts."

"We could do that, Papa," Kris interjected, eager to contribute something to the conversation. The hairs on the back of his neck were still prickling from Davey's account of his friend's scalping.

"We just might," Hans agreed.

"Well, I must be going." Davey told them. "I'd like to say good-bye to Sheila before I go."

"She is busy," Maddy said curtly.

"Surely she can come to the steps and say farewell," Davey insisted. "I hate to leave without saying good-bye to her. It wouldn't be polite."

Hans and Maddy exchanged looks. Hans shrugged. Maddy had opened her mouth to say something, when they all heard a yelp from inside the unfinished house. Davey looked up and saw Sheila peering over the top of the front wall.

"Look," she shrieked. "Indians." She pointed to the south. Maddy, Kris, and Hans all looked past Davey and their eyes widened in fright. Kris reached for his rifle, snatching it away from the porch. Hans picked up his own rifle and stuck the flint and leather inside the jaws of the clamp.

Davey turned slowly and saw the band of Indians riding toward them along the wide buffalo trail that bordered the Platte River. His eyes narrowed as the Indians fanned out and began to whoop, brandishing war clubs and spears above their heads.

Maddy screamed in terror and picked up her hoe.

"We're all going to die," she shouted.

Chapter Eleven

The small band of Indians rode quickly out of the mist rising off the river. As they fanned out, the brume parted and spun off in the wake of their ponies like gossamer smoke. Their faces were not painted, but they wore eagle feathers that dangled from their scalp locks and spun with the wind.

Davey turned to Hans and his son. "Put those rifles away."

"We will defend ourselves," Hans said, in his heavy accent.

"Put the rifles away. Those are Arapaho."

"I do not trust them," Maddy said, still gripping the handle of the hoe.

"If you want to live to see another sunset, ma'am, you'll make your men put away their weapons." Davey looked at the woman with piercing eyes, hard as agates. Sheila ventured outside the walls of the dwelling and stood in the doorway. Her fair hair flowed around her shoulders like a delicate shawl.

Hans and Kris set their rifles down, but within easy reaching distance. Davey turned toward the oncoming riders and raised his empty right hand. The leader switched his war club to his left hand and raised his right in reply.

"Do you know that man?" Hans asked.

"I know him. They call him Eagle Heart. We've had some dealings."

"Hans—" Maddy started to say.

"Be quiet," Hans interrupted as the Arapaho braves started shrieking and calling out. Kris backed toward his rifle, his face contorted in fear. Maddy put both hands to her heart and sidled toward her husband. Sheila watched in rapt fascination as the buckskin-clad Arapaho drew closer.

Davey waited, his hand still upheld, palm facing Eagle Heart and his companions.

The Groots shrank back toward the dwelling as the Arapaho braves rode up at a gallop and reined their ponies to a stop a few yards from where Davey stood. The leader, Eagle Heart, spoke to the trapper in his native tongue.

"Hello, friend. You have some good furs. Do you trade here with these white faces?"

"No," Davey replied in Arapaho. "These are people from where the sun rises. They grow food from seeds they plant in the ground."

"Why are they in this place?"

"They say the earth is good here."

"The earth is good for the buffalo, for the Arapaho. The white man does not belong here."

"They wish to live here in peace with the Arapaho."

Eagle Heart looked at the Groots first, studying each of their faces. Then he looked at Sheila for several seconds, until her face flushed with embarrassment.

"Flame Hair," the brave said, bestowing the sobriquet on Sheila.

"Shee-la," Davey said.

"Shee-la," Eagle Heart repeated, his mouth curving into a grin. "Very pretty," he added, in Arapaho.

Davey said nothing.

"Do these white faces have gifts for Eagle Heart?" The

warrior looked into Hans's face, his own visage without expression.

Davey turned to Hans Groot. "Eagle Heart wants to know if you have gifts for him and his braves. He does speak some English, by the way."

"What does he want?" Hans asked.

"I expect he could use some tobacco, coffee, sugar, maybe some powder and ball."

"I do not see any rifles."

"This is the small advance party of Arapaho, come to find summer camp for the tribe. But if you look real close, under those buffalo robes on the backs of their ponies, you'll see where they have their rifles stowed."

Hans glanced at the buffalo robes, carefully folded and tied with leather thongs to a kind of cinch under the bellies of the ponies.

"I do not like to give Indians powder and lead," he said nervously.

"You will want to make friends with these braves. They might be willing to help you someday."

"How could they help me?"

"They hate Utes," Davey replied.

"Well, I will give them some of what we have. After all, we expected this one day."

"Good." Davey nodded. "I will tell Eagle Heart that you will give him some of what you have."

"Tell him I do not have much."

Davey nodded again, turned to Eagle Heart. Hans barked orders to Sheila and Maddy, but it was Sheila who turned to enter the dwelling first. Eagle Heart watched her, and so did another brave, Crow Pipe, a scowl on his face that was permanent. A scar down his cheek crossed the corner of his mouth, so that he appeared to be frowning all the time. But his eyes glittered in their sockets like bright obsidian beads swimming in lamp oil.

The others spoke sotto voce among themselves. Davey knew them: Big Bull, Spotted Hawk, Black Knife, and Scatters the Deer. They were all virile young men, full of vitality, with scars and nicks on their bodies from battle and sacred rituals. They seemed to Davey like a bunch of boys out riding on a Sunday afternoon, with not a care in the world. But he knew they were aware of their surroundings and were not so carefree as they appeared. Scatters, for all his seeming idleness, kept his eyes on the mountain range and Spotted Hawk watched the prairie around them, while Big Bull glanced along the riverbank every few seconds.

Within moments Sheila emerged from the dwelling, her arms laden with tins of coffee and sacks of sugar. She carried flour sacks and laid them alongside the food staples on the porch. Maddy came outside a few seconds later with tobacco twists and leaves, some candies, and a box of flints. Hans nodded to Kris, who disappeared around the corner of the house. He returned with sacks of lead balls and some lead ingots.

"Whiskey," said Eagle Heart in English.

"No whiskey," Hans said. "Candies my wife made."

"Knives," Eagle Heart continued. "Hatchets."

"We have no knives to spare," Hans said. "No hatchets but those we use ourselves."

Davey explained this to the Arapaho leader, who seemed satisfied.

Eagle Heart then pointed to Sheila and signed to Davey. Hans watched the exchange with a look of apprehension on his face.

"What's he saying?" the settler asked.

Davey smiled. "He wonders how many ponies you will take for the blond-haired girl."

"He wants to buy Sheila?"

"Yes."

"She is not for sale," Hans said.

"He also asks if she is a slave."

"What did you tell him?" Hans demanded, bristling.

"I told him nothing."

"Then what does he mean by that?"

"Eagle Heart is very observant," was Davey's only response.

"She is not a slave," Hans said.

"Don't lie, Mr. Groot. These Indians don't take to lying."

"I am not lying. She is a bondservant, legally bound to me. She is a member of our family."

Sheila's eyes widened. Eagle Heart signed to Davey, who explained as best he could the arrangement Hans had with Sheila's mother.

"She is a slave," Eagle Heart repeated in Arapaho.

Davey nodded.

"I will buy her from the white eyes someday," Eagle Heart announced in English. Then he spoke to the others, and they dismounted and gathered up the goods on the porch and put the coffee and sugar in flour and seed sacks and tied these to their ponies.

"We come back," Eagle Heart said to Hans. "I buy Sun Hair. Bring many ponies, buffalo robes."

With that, the Arapaho chief and the other braves mounted and rode off without looking back. Davey watched them go and knew that the Groots were forever bound to this bunch of Arapaho.

"What did he say to you before he said he'd come back?" Hans asked.

"He said he understood about Sheila being a part of your family."

"Then why will he come back to buy her?"

"I don't know." Davey shrugged. "You'll have to ask him when he returns."

"I hope I never see him again," Hans said.

"They will make summer camp a short distance up the

South Platte," Davey said. "They'll be kind of like neigh-
bors, sort of."

Maddy snorted in disgust. Sheila smiled and then hid
the smile behind her hand as she looked at Davey. Hans
grunted and said, "Come, we must get to work. Good day to
you, Mr. Longworth."

"I'll be seeing you," Davey said, and walked away.
That's when he saw the smoke signals appearing on two
ridges some distance apart. One came from nearby, somewhere along the Cache de la Poudre, the other from a spot
that was near or on Lookout Mountain, in the direction he
was going.

"What does that smoke mean?" Hans asked as Davey
was mounting his horse.

"Could be talk about Eagle Heart and his braves."

"It is the Utes?"

"I reckon," Davey said. "Keep your eyes peeled. If the
Utes come by, it won't be for tobacco and sugar."

"What do you mean?" Maddy asked.

"Likely it will be for your scalps," Davey told her, and
clucked to his horse. He waved to Sheila and she smiled and
waved back.

Davey watched the balls of smoke rising at intervals
into the blue sky. If there was trouble at the Groots', he
thought, it would happen soon.

Chapter Twelve

avey saw the riders break over the ridge at Lookout Mountain. They formed a line of horses and pack mules laden with furs. But the minute he spotted the small caravan, he knew something was wrong. The horses were running and the pack mules were striving hard to keep up.

He recognized the trapper in the lead. He had no doubt that it was Fritz Stamm, the very man who had accompanied him to Jefferson Territory three years before. He and Fritz had lasted a season together before realizing that they could not get along through a winter in the isolated snow-flocked mountains.

The cool north breeze had been at his back all morning and now the wind shifted, so that it came from the south, and he could smell the thawing earth and the fresh scent of snow still on the hillsides. He kicked his horse in the flanks to pick up speed. The column of trappers were racing headlong down the slope of the foothill now and he chose a path to intersect them. As he rode up a rise the riders disappeared and that's when he saw why they were running so hard. Above them, on a slender ridge, Davey saw other riders, wearing eagle plumes in their dark hair and firing arrows from their bows down at the trappers.

He marveled at the horsemanship of the Indians, but they were still too far away for him to see what tribe they claimed. But he knew without seeing that they were not Arapaho. As he topped the ridge he was almost certain that they were Utes, and his stomach churned. There were only a half dozen of them, but they had the high ground and they were raining arrows down at the caravan from full quivers.

Davey heard sounds of gunfire, the crack of rifles from somewhere in the draw where the trappers had gone. He saw puffs of smoke rising in the air, billowing up toward the ridge where the attacking Indians were riding back and forth, shooting arrows down to where Fritz and the other trappers must have ridden.

Another rattle of rifle fire and the Indians scattered as one of their number fell from his pony. Davey drew his rifle as he neared another rise. He was still too far away for a shot, but once he cleared the small knoll, he'd be within range. White smoke floated up from the draw and then dissipated in the gentle breeze.

All day long, Davey had seen the smoke and the mirrors and he knew something had stirred up the Utes. He'd seen the signals and had wondered how many Utes were talking to each other over great distances. Now men he knew were under attack by one band of Indians, Utes most probably, and he'd bet a packet of furs they were painted for war.

Davey topped the knoll and rode down a broad swale through long grasses that ticked his boot moccasins. And then he saw the band of trappers spread out along the draw, huddled against the bank, looking up for targets. He watched as the Utes snuck along the ridge out of sight to a point lower down. For the time being, the trappers were safe, but a couple of yards farther down the trail, they'd sure as hell run into an ambush.

Davey checked his rifle, made sure the pan was primed,

the flint secure in its leather patch. He rode down the gentle slope and yelled to the closest man he saw.

The man turned and started to throw down on Davey, but then recognized him and pulled his rifle back and held it at his waist. One of the Indians in the rear of the pack spotted Davey and gestured to his fellow braves. They began to shoot arrows at him and he rode through a hail of shafts that pronged the ground around him. But none found its mark and Davey reached the draw, out of breath, his horse whistling through its nostrils, the mules straining to keep up and breathe at the same time.

"Ho, Davey," called one of the trappers, a man called Peaches. His real name was Beecham, but nicknames were common among men who had no use for titles or formal names.

"Hold up," Davey said, and then saw Fritz Stamm stick his head up from behind a small boulder.

"You come at a bad time," Fritz said. "Better take cover."

"They're fixin' to ambush you further down the draw," Davey said, swinging off his horse. "Utes, are they?"

"They're Utes all right," Peaches confirmed. "Been chasin' us nigh onto four—five mile."

"How come?" Davey asked.

"I don't reckon we know." Fritz looked over Davey's bundles of furs on the mules as he spoke. "Jumped us at a creek up yonder and kilt Jasper Rydell, the kid."

Davey remembered Jasper. Fritz had taken him on as a partner, against his better judgment, last summer. He was a snaggletoothed, skinny kid with not much sense and few clothes on his back. But he'd had his traps and an old musket and a new hatchet. Davey had been surprised that Fritz would give such a kid a sugar tit after their experiences up in the mountains. They had gotten on each other's nerves shortly after the first big snow and had not spoken more than a few words to each other the rest of the winter.

"Sorry to hear about it," Davey said. "I see them bucks got paint on their faces."

"Yeah," Peaches said. "We saw 'em makin' smoke talk all mornin' but never figgered they'd jump us. Hell, we was aleavin' anyway."

The other trappers who had gathered around laughed nervously, and some of them kept looking up to the top of the ridge.

"What do you make of it, Davey?" asked Fritz. "You run into any renegade Utes?"

"Not really. But Caleb Wakefield bought him some ground up on the Poudre. Three of 'em shot him and scalped him down on the South Platte, chased him back up to where I was."

"Dead?" Fritz asked.

"Yeah, he died," Davey said.

There was a silence in the group. Davey looked at the men. They seemed haggard, all red-eyed and gaunt from a rough winter. Some of them looked scared, too. There was Giblets and Frenchie and Tall Tom and Beaver Face, another man he didn't know, a couple of youngsters he had barely met the previous summer.

"Well, you'd best ride out on the plain," Davey told them. "You keep goin' down this draw and you'll have Utes all over you like seed ticks."

"Much obliged," Peaches said. "Just how in the hell do we get back up on high ground without makin' targets of ourselves?"

"You got a point." Davey frowned. The draw was steep, and while they climbed out of it at any point for a mile or so either way, they would be in full view of the Utes. He studied the draw and figured where the Utes would be waiting.

"Well, no sense in heading back where you come from,"

he told Fritz. "And if you keep on your course for Cherry Creek, you'll catch hob."

"We can't wait 'em out neither," said Tall Tom. "Them rascals has already kilt one of us and they've got blood in their eyes."

"If we let them flank us from the east, we'd be trapped," Peaches offered.

"Right," Davey said. "Best thing to do is ride the side-hill up to the flat. Leave the pack animals here. Then we can flank 'em ourselves and drive 'em off."

"Sounds right to me," Fritz commented, and the others murmured in agreement.

"One more thing," Davey began.

"What?" asked Frenchie.

"Somebody in your bunch dropped one of their braves when I rode up."

"So? That bother you?" Tall Tom asked.

"No," Davey said.

"Good," one of the men muttered.

"Maybe not so good," Davey said. "If the Utes were stirred up before, they'll be hopping mad now. Maybe we ought to just ride off and let 'em be."

"You sound like a goddamned Injun lover," Frenchie spat. "We heard you was pretty thick with them redskins."

Davey glanced at Fritz, who turned away for a moment, avoiding eye contact. Well, that had been a thing between them, the time they wintered in the mountains. Davey had made friends with Eagle Heart and his band and it had made Fritz mighty nervous. They had argued about white men and red for days, neither of them willing to concede the other's point. Davey felt that they owed the red man something for the use of his land, the plundering of his beaver, and Fritz, like most white men, thought that the Indians were nothing but homeless savages with no right to land they didn't hold paper on.

"You boys do what you want," Davey told them. "I'm just sayin' the Utes have been making smoke and talking with mirrors for days and now you say they're painted for war. I think this little war party is just a parry, a way to test our strength. If you draw blood, just be sure you can pay the consequences."

"You're damned right," Peaches said. "We ain't goin' to let them thievin' Utes get away with what they done. I say we go after 'em and skin some hide."

"Better be about it, then," Davey said. He started to ground-tie his mules and the others followed suit.

"Should we leave someone behind to guard the furs?" Tall Tom asked.

"No need. We'll either come back and get 'em or we won't," Davey said.

There was muttering and grumbling among the trappers, but they all tied their mules and checked their rifles. Davey led the way, riding a long angle up the sidehill to gain the high ground. When they were all on the top, he kicked his horse. The band of trappers charged along the prairie straight at the place where the Utes waited.

"Looks like we'll get us a fight," Peaches observed, riding up next to Davey.

"Looks like. I counted a half dozen. How about you?"

"Well, seemed like more. They run us into that draw deliberately, and then I thought I heard some of 'em ride off like."

"Ride off?"

"Heard them soft pony hooves and I don't know where the rest of 'em run off to."

Davey cursed.

"What's the matter?" Fritz asked, having overheard the last part of the conversation.

"We may be running into more than a handful of Utes,"

Davey answered. "Peaches here said there were more of 'em when they chased you down the draw."

"That's right," Fritz confirmed. "We run the rest off. These are just hardheads, boys wantin' to count coup."

"You think so?" Davey looked dubious.

"Why, sure."

"I hope to hell you're right, Fritz."

Just then Tall Tom cried out and they all saw the five Utes on the other side of the draw. They were making crude gestures with their hands, exposing their genitals by lifting their breechcloths, and brandishing their bows.

"It looks too easy," Davey observed.

"Come on boys, let's get them bastards," yelled Peaches, and raced ahead of the column of trappers.

Davey tried to stop the men, but it was too late. And then he saw the trap open wide. Utes rose up out of the tall prairie grasses on either side of the advancing mountain men, arrows nocked to their bowstrings.

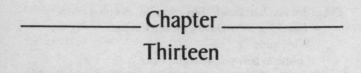

D avey called out to the men riding up ahead of him. At the same time he saw that each Ute had his arrow pointing to a different man. They meant to wipe out the whole party at once.

"Swing left," Davey cried, and saw Peaches turn his horse to the north just as a Ute loosed an arrow in his direction. He heard the whick, whick, of bowstrings releasing their lethal shafts. The trappers scattered like a covey of flushed quail and began firing their rifles.

Fortunately, the shots went wide of their marks, and the Utes nocked their second arrows so fast it was all a blur. Davey picked out the nearest Ute and drew a tight bead on him as his horse held to a line he had chosen. He squeezed the trigger and saw the Ute throw up his hands and stagger back with the force of the lead ball. The warrior's bow dropped from his hands as he fell on his back.

Meanwhile the Utes on the other side of the draw started down the slope to ride to the other side. Davey knew that if they came to the aid of their brethren, the fight could well be lost. He reloaded quickly, something he had practiced a lot during the long winters in the mountains, and called to Fritz. "Get two men and follow me."

The trappers had their hands full. The Utes were seasoned warriors and they dodged lead balls as they continued to keep up a steady flow of arrows. But the mountain men were not easy targets on horseback.

Dodging flying arrows, Fritz rounded up Tall Tom and Peaches and followed Davey to the rim of the draw.

"We can't let 'em get across," Davey said. "Watch your backs."

Some of the Utes on foot turned to attack the four men riding to cut off the mounted Ute braves. Davey swung around and set his sight on the nearest brave. "Take 'em," he shouted to Fritz. Then he squeezed off a shot and watched a crimson flower blossom on the charging Ute's chest. He crumpled, snapping his bow in half as he fell. Davey heard the crackle of rifles as Peaches, Fritz and Tall Tom raked the Utes with lead ball and shot. Utes collapsed in the tall grasses and disappeared from sight.

"Now reload quickly," Davey ordered. "Here come the others."

With that, he turned his horse back toward the draw and the others did the same. Behind them, they could hear the sporadic snap of locks and the crack of rifles, but they had no way of knowing if any of the shots hit home. Davey had the eerie feeling that he could find himself with an arrow between the shoulder blades at any moment, or a stray ball in the back of his head. But he quelled his apprehension and reloaded, not remembering whether he had already done so in the heat of the fight.

Meanwhile the Utes who had been on the other side of the draw had fanned out and were scrambling down the slope into the bottom. In a few moments they would be in range.

"Wait until they're less than a hundred yards from us," Davey told the men. "And remember, you're shooting downhill. Watch your windage."

"Damn right," Peaches said.

"Maybe get 'em on the upslope," Tall Tom suggested.

Fritz nodded. "That would be good." Davey knew that they were talking to keep up their courage. It was unnerving to sit their horses and listen to the sounds of battle behind them.

As if putting a name to his fears, Davey heard a rustling behind him and the *swish, swish,* of flapping grasses. Half turning, he glimpsed a Ute running toward him.

"Davey, look out," Fritz cried, swinging his rifle toward the approaching warrior.

Knowing that Fritz's shot would be too late, Davey twisted in the saddle and leveled his rifle barrel at the Ute and squeezed off a shot. He missed the man, who threw his war club at him and then ran off. The warrior stopped suddenly and made an obscene gesture, lifting his breechcloth and exposing his genitals. Davey calmly reloaded and did not respond.

"Here they come," Tall Tom called, and brought his rifle to his shoulder. Davey looked down into the draw and saw that the Utes were at the bottom. In a few seconds they would be climbing up the near side, which would put them within killing range.

His stomach roiled as he thought about killing the Utes down in the draw. It seemed such a waste of human life. Yet he knew the Utes wanted to kill him. He just wished there was a better way to resolve the situation. His palms grew sweaty. The Utes seemed in no hurry. Peaches kept cocking and uncocking the lock on his rifle. Davey glanced at Tall Tom, who was licking his lips as if they were dry. Fritz was hunched over the saddle, his rifle to his shoulder, sighting along the barrel.

"Fritz, what do you think?" Davey whispered.

"It looks too easy," Fritz replied.

"Like shootin' fish in a bar'l," Peaches whispered tightly.

"Seems a damned shame," Davey said.

"Maybe you *are* an Injun lover," Tall Tom put in.

"They don't stand a chance," Davey said.

"Well, they were atryin' to lift our hair," Tall Tom reminded him.

Peaches harrumphed. "Damned sure was."

Suddenly the advancing Utes in the draw stopped moving. One of them looked up and Davey felt a strong compulsion to wave at him. But the Ute made no sign, and for a moment time seemed to stand still.

"What the hell?" Fritz said.

Davey said nothing. Then he heard a cry from behind and the sound of hoofbeats. He turned and saw Utes on horseback closing in on the other trappers. But they weren't shooting arrows. They were leading barebacked ponies and galloping at full speed, the braves hugging the flanks of their mounts so that they were barely visible.

"Look out," Frenchie cried, and even as he called out, the Utes on foot disappeared below the high grasses. Then in a startling display of horsemanship, the oncoming Utes scattered and rode toward the hidden men. They slowed their ponies slightly and the Utes on foot rose up and climbed onto the riderless ponies. They seemed to flow onto the backs of their mounts in a single fluid motion.

The trappers were caught by surprise and watched as the Utes, all mounted now, rode off, hugging the sides of their ponies so that they were smaller targets. Pairs of Utes picked up their dead, working in complete harmony, so that their ponies barely slowed as each man reached down and grabbed the arms of a slain warrior. The rescue was accomplished so deftly and gracefully that they seemed to melt away without a shot being fired from either side.

When Davey turned around and looked down into the draw, the Utes there were riding off, out of rifle range, down to the end of the gully.

Peaches, Fritz, and Tall Tom also watched as the Utes rode off, heading for the open prairie. Their forms became smaller and smaller and they were met at the open end by the Utes who had rescued their fellow braves from the open plain.

"There they go," Fritz said.

"But will they come back?" Tall Tom asked.

Davey shrugged. He didn't know. The fight now seemed like a dream to him. The plain was deserted of fighting Utes and the draw empty. He felt a silence wash over him and the tension in his stomach subsided. It had been a thrilling sight and his respect for the Indians rose. Truly, the Utes were a formidable enemy. They could have overcome the trappers had they wanted to, he felt, but they chose to leave the field of battle to fight another day. Davey took their actions as a warning. True, he had killed, but he had not conquered.

"It's over," he stated flatly.

"It don't make no sense." Peaches' tone was thick with shock and wonder.

"They got scared is all," Tall Tom opined. "We beat 'em."

"Maybe," Fritz said.

Davey said nothing. He knew the Indians had not lost their courage. They had surely had a purpose in attacking the trappers in the first place. And they had been well organized. The second band of Utes had been waiting on the prairie, out of sight, ready to ride to the rescue at the first hint of trouble.

Still, it was all puzzling. It was obvious to him that the Indians had planned the entire action with care, had tracked the trappers, and meant to kill them if they could. But they had held some of the band in reserve. He marveled at the generalship of the Ute leader.

"What do you think now, Davey?" Fritz asked as he rode up close.

"I think we got beat."

"We didn't lose a man," Fritz said proudly.

"No, but every one of us has a scar now, and something else."

"What's that?"

"Fear," Davey replied. "That was only a small band. If the Utes ever come at us in strength, they'll wipe us out."

"I'm not afraid," Fritz said.

"You should be," Davey told him. "Those Utes there, they just declared war on the white man."

Fritz looked out on the plain. There was not a Ute to be seen. But Davey's words struck him, and deep down, he knew the other trapper was right. The fear *was* there. He could feel his heart pounding in his chest, echoing the drumbeats of war.

Chapter Fourteen

Hans Groot had thought a lot about the trapper and the Indians since Davey's departure two days before. He resented those who minded other people's business. He did not like intruders; indeed, he mistrusted most people. But Davey worried him more than most. He had paid undue attention to Sheila, and he was friendly with the savages. And there was another thing that bothered Hans about Davey—he had pried into the matter of Sheila's bondservancy.

"Send Sheila to fetch some more wood," Hans ordered Maddy.

"But I need her here. We have plenty of firewood."

"I want to talk to you and Kris."

Maddy sighed. "Of course, my husband."

Hans called to his son, who was fixing the mule's harness. Sheila was scrubbing clothes in a large vat of steaming water and lye soapsuds. "Kris, you come," Hans said.

"Yes, Papa."

Maddy walked over to Sheila, who did not look up. She was stirring the clothes with a peeled tree limb. Her blond hair was askew, locks dangling over her freckled face. She was sweating in the morning sun, her too-small clothes tight against her fulsome body.

"Yes'm," Sheila said, without looking up.

"You are to fetch wood," Maddy demanded coldly.

"But I am doing the washing,"

"Don't sass me, Sheila. Do as I say."

"When I finish?"

"Now," Maddy said. "And no more arguing from you."

"Yes'm." Sheila left the pole in the soapy water and wiped her face free of perspiration. She looked over at the woodpile. There was enough for a week or more of cooking, washing, and firelight. She caught a glimpse of Maddy watching her suspiciously.

"Be quick about it," the older woman added.

"I have to walk a long way for wood," Sheila protested.

"Then you will have to walk a long way. Now go."

"Yes'm," Sheila said. "Will you be finishing the washing, then?"

"You will finish when you return," Maddy told her curtly.

"It might be nigh dark when I get back."

Maddy slapped her across the mouth. Sheila recoiled in pain and surprise, bringing a hand up to her mouth. The slap stung and had brought stars to her eyes.

"Maybe you'll learn to mind me, Sheila, without a lot of backtalk."

"But, I wasn't—"

Maddy slapped her again, this time on the side of the face. The force of the blow turned Sheila's head.

"I'm going, ma'am," she said, not looking at the older woman. But sparks of anger flashed in her eyes, narrowed in hatred for the cruel woman who had struck her.

"You had better," Maddy said.

Sheila half ran, half walked to the woodshed. When she was out of sight, Hans turned to Maddy and Kris, "Let's go inside and talk."

Hans's wife and son followed him into the partially finished house. Gradually, the dwelling was becoming more livable, with all the walls up and part of the roof completed. Hans figured they would be finished within a week or less.

The Groots sat at the table where they had eaten breakfast that morning before the sun was up. After the chairs stopped scraping, Hans cleared his throat.

"I am worried about that trapper fellow," he began. "I do not like him. I do not like him prying."

"He is gone, my husband," Maddy said.

"But he said he will be back. And those Indians. They will be back as well."

"What do you want to do, Papa?" Kris asked.

"I think we had better be prepared to get rid of these people. Make it so that they will no longer bother us."

Maddy looked at him questioningly. "How do we do that?"

"When the Indians return, we do not give them anything. When that Davey returns, we do not talk to him."

"You tried that," Maddy said.

Hans's face flushed under his wife's criticism. "I did what I thought was best. I knew he was a snooper and sometimes you let them snoop and they go away."

"But you think he will come back. So?"

"He knows that Sheila is bonded to me."

There was a silence at the table. Maddy looked at her son. Kris lowered his head.

"Maybe we should sell her," Maddy suggested.

"We need her," Hans said.

"If the trapper finds out . . ." Maddy did not finish her sentence, because there was no need. Hans and Kris knew what she meant.

"It could be trouble," Hans admitted.

"Sheila might find out," Kris said.

Hans glared at his son. Kris did not avoid his father's gaze, but stared back, unblinking.

"How would she find out?" Hans asked, his voice leaden as a falling sash weight. "You will tell her, maybe?"

"Not me," Kris replied quickly. "But she might find out."

"The bond should have been for ten years," Maddy said, trying to mollify her husband.

"Well, we do not know where her mother is. The girl is better off with us." Hans seemed to be trying to convince himself of the rightness of his actions. He knew he did not sound convincing.

"She doesn't think so," Kris said.

"You think she will run away?" Hans said.

Kris shrugged.

"Or someone will take her away," Maddy said. "Maybe that trapper."

"Maybe that Indian, Eagle Heart," Kris added quickly.

Hans pounded his fist on the table. "No," he said loudly. "They will not take her. I will not allow it."

"But how can you stop them, my husband?" Maddy wanted to know.

Hans dropped his head into his open hands. "I don't know," he muttered.

"There is one way we won't have to worry that Sheila's bond is paid," Kris said, after an empty moment.

Hans lifted his head from his hands and looked at his son. Kris looked away, as if wondering if he had gone too far.

"Tell me," Hans said softly.

"If Sheila and I were to be married, then we would be able to keep her."

"It would be legal then," Maddy agreed.

"You have talked about this with your mother?" Hans asked.

"Well, a little," Kris admitted.

Hans's lips bent into a frown of distaste. "You would be marrying beneath you, my son."

"Yes, but we would not have to worry about the bond that has run out."

Hans looked at Maddy, who said nothing, but her expression was beseeching. She brushed a strand of hair away from her face as if to emphasize her determination to stand up to her husband, if necessary.

"This would be a big price to pay," Hans said, glancing from Maddy to Kris.

"But we would not have to worry about someone finding out that Sheila is no longer bound to us," Maddy said quickly. "Sheila would be Kris's wife and . . ."

"And be part of our family," Hans finished for her, disgust in his tone.

"Yes." Maddy let her head drop until she was staring at the table.

"You would do this for us?" Hans asked, looking at Kris.

"I would."

"You would sleep with her?"

Kris swallowed hard, but that did not keep the blood from rising to his face. "Well . . ." he began.

"We will have to go to the other settlers and speak to them," Hans said. "We will have to ask one of the elders to marry you and Sheila."

"I think Peter van der Meer can do this," Maddy said.

Hans pondered for several moments as his wife and son seemingly held their breaths. "This we will do," he said at last. "In a month, when we have finished the house and the planting."

Maddy and Kris both breathed sighs of relief.

"Thank you, my husband," Maddy said.

"There will be a marriage," Hans told her, "if that girl lives long enough."

Chapter
Fifteen

Cherry Creek wasn't much of a settlement. It was only a gathering place for trappers, prospectors, drifters, and dreamers. But a cheer rose up along the banks of the creek as Davey, Fritz, and the others rode up late in the afternoon, their mules laden with fur pelts garnered in the Rocky Mountains.

Tall Tom could not hold back from telling his story about the Utes. He immediately climbed from the saddle and began telling it all, in detail. Several men left their digs and gathered around him. Soon the other trappers joined the conversation, leaving Davey and Fritz alone.

"Where's the buyer from Bent's?" Davey asked when a man passed them on his way to hear the news from Tall Tom and the others.

"Yonder." The man pointed upstream. "Name of Gwaltney."

"Obliged." Davey nodded.

"I'll ride over with you, Davey," Fritz offered. His tone implied that he wanted to talk to Davey, not just keep him company.

The two men passed through a makeshift settlement consisting of lean-tos, tents, hastily thrown-up wooden structures that were at best ramshackle shelters, hovels made of deadwood limbs and bark. Some of the cookfires were blazing and there was a commingling of smells that defied recognition, but Davey drew in the tangy aroma.

"Makes a man hungry," Fritz said.

"Or makes him throw up," Davey said dryly.

"You don't like people much, do you, Davey?"

"I like 'em all right. I just don't put much stock in most."

"Always wondered about you when we was partnering that winter. Why'd you hook up with me? Me being older and all."

"I trusted you, Fritz."

"Why?"

"You probably reminded me of my father, or my uncle Samuel."

"Good men?"

"No, but honest," Davey said. "Honest as any, I reckon. And dependable when it counted."

"You make quick judgments of men, eh? Are you always right?"

"I'm usually pretty close," Davey said.

"There is something big on your mind today, huh?"

"You mean the Utes?"

"No, that's big enough. But when I first saw you, well, maybe I'm wrong. . . ."

"About what?"

"You looked like you was worried or something. Maybe watching Caleb die gave you a shiver?"

"I hated to see him die like that," Davey admitted.

"But that's not what's bothering you, eh, Davey?" Fritz pressed.

"I guess I've been thinking about a girl I met up on the Platte a couple of days ago."

"White girl?"

Davey nodded. "More like a slave girl." He explained

his discovery of the settlers, of Sheila Stewart's status as a bondservant. He also told Fritz about the Arapaho visit, and Eagle Heart's offer to buy the girl from the Groot family.

"It's none of our business," Fritz concluded as they passed through the camp toward a fire blazing among the trees, well away from the creek bank.

"It might be, Fritz. Those people picked a bad place and time to homestead. And I don't hold with slavery."

"All perfectly legal, Davey. The girl's bonded out to them, you say?"

"She says she's eighteen. They bought her when she was twelve. That's a long time for servitude. And from the looks of things, the Groots work her pretty damned hard."

"Maybe she's bound to them for ten years."

"Could be," Davey allowed. "As you say, it's really none of my business."

"But it bothers you. You take a likin' to the gal?"

Davey sighed. "I don't know. I been thinkin' of her."

"Then you took a likin' to her," Fritz said.

Davey did not reply. He had been thinking of Sheila almost constantly. Worrying might be a better term, he decided. The Utes were on the warpath and the Groots were sitting right on the great buffalo migration trail. The Arapahos hated the Utes, and the Utes hated the whites and the Arapahos. If there was going to be a war, then Sheila might be caught in the middle.

But what could he do about that? He didn't know how he felt about Sheila just yet. He didn't like the idea of her being bound to such a family, but they had their rights, he supposed. And it wasn't right for him to interfere. Unless Sheila asked him to. He would have to talk to her and see if she was content to let things be.

Davey shook his head as if to clear it of thoughts he could not control. Whatever situation the Groots might find themselves in, there was nothing he could do about it now.

"Looks like we're first in," Fritz observed as the two men rode into the circle of firelight.

Bill Gwaltney waved to them. He stood behind make-shift tables fashioned from green whipsawed lumber set atop tree stumps. He was a tall, dark man—some said he was mulatto—and he drew on a long cigar, expelling bluish smoke when he exhaled.

"Fritz, Davey." Bill nodded. "You boys trap together this year?"

"No," Fritz said. "You know."

Bill nodded again, his dark eyes glittering in the glow of the orange fire. Nearby stood a fur press and a large roll of twine. There was a scale at the end of one table, sitting on the ground, lead weights stacked neatly on a keg of black powder.

Davey dismounted, ground-tied his horse, and led the mules toward the rim of the circle of light. Fritz rode to the other side and dismounted. Davey began untying the dia-mond hitches that held the panniers in place on the mules' backs.

"What's all the ruckus about over by the creek?" Gwalt-ney asked.

"Me and some others ran into Utes up by Lookout Mountain. They ragged us most all winter, kilt a kid."

"Too bad." Bill grimaced.

"It's going to get worse," Fritz said.

"How's Charles doing?" Davey asked. "And Ceran, William?"

"William's gone to Santa Fe. Charles bought out St. Vrain, I reckon. He's tryin' to sell the fort."

"Sell the fort?" Fritz asked, incredulous. "To who?"

"He says to the army. Means to do it, too."

Davey scratched his head. "Things change mighty fast," he commented.

"Too fast, sometimes," Fritz said. Gwaltney drew on his cigar and blew out a spool of smoke, then laughed, shaking his head.

"Who's first?" Bill asked.

"You go ahead, Davey," Fritz said. "I ain't in no particular hurry."

"Let's see what you brung, Davey," Bill said. "Bring your packets over to the table."

Bill put on a pair of spectacles. He lit a lantern at the end of the table, turned the wick up so that glaring light spilled onto his work area, then snubbed out his cigar and stuck the butt into his shirt pocket.

"I'll give you a hand," Fritz offered.

The two men carried the packets over to the table and laid them atop the empty surface. Gwaltney cut the sinew binding one packet and began examining the pelts.

"Prime," he said.

"They're all prime," Davey told him. "And I've got more such cached."

Gwaltney riffled thorugh the furs in each packet, counting, writing down the tally in a ledger. Sometimes he would pick up a pelt and sniff it, run his fingers through the fur, and stretch the hide while looking at the inside. He was swift and meticulous in his survey.

"What are you paying?" Davey asked.

"Four," Gwaltney said.

"Five."

"Four-fifty."

"Four seventy-five."

Bill huffed in a breath. "I'll give you four-sixty."

"Weigh 'em, Bill," Davey said.

"Help me lug them to the press, will you?" Gwaltney asked.

The three men carried the furs to the press. Bill

compressed the furs into tight, compact bundles, weighed
them on the scales, and logged the weight of each packet,
then tagged them with coded numbers.

Gwaltney was just paying Davey for the furs when the
three men heard a volley of shots from downstream. The
next thing they knew men had begun yelling and they heard
the pounding of boots and moccasins on the ground.

"What the hell?" Fritz swung his head around to see
what was happening.

"Trouble, likely," Bill said.

"I'd bet on it." Davey took the gold coins from the
trader.

There was no more shooting, but the shouting and yelling had intensified.

"We'd better take a look-see, Davey," Fritz said.

"I'll go with you," Gwaltney offered.

Davey nodded. Bill put his strongbox away with the
furs, making sure it was padlocked. The three men grabbed
their rifles and headed downstream at a jog. When they had
gone about two hundred yards, they saw a group of men carrying torches. Everyone seemed to be talking at once.

The sky was gradually paling as the sun fell to the rim
of the western peaks and the creek glistened with a golden
glow. Several men ran to their lean-tos and tents, grabbed
up rifles as Davey, Fritz, and Bill passed them on their way
to the scene of the commotion.

"A fight?" Fritz asked.

"Who knows," Bill said.

When they reached the crowd, Davey saw that most of
them were looking at two men laid out on the ground. Both
were covered with blood, their buckskin shirts soaked. One
man's skull was cracked open like a ripe melon.

Bill Gwaltney gagged.

"Hey, Davey," called Peaches. "Looky here."

"What's going on?" Davey asked.

"Utes. They done kilt two more men and four more got arrers in 'em."

Peaches stepped outside the circle of men. His face was bone white.

Another man stepped onto a stump and stood above the crowd. He called for silence.

"Who's that?" Davey asked.

Bill Gwaltney stopped dead in his tracks. "That's a man you don't want to know, Davey. Name's John Cleel. And they don't come any more rotten."

Davey looked at Cleel. He was a tall, rangy man with a florid face; at the moment he was patting the air with his hands.

"Listen up," he called.

Before he could say another word, a man staggered from the crowd, choking on blood. He took three steps and fell down dead. The crowd gasped. Blood poured from the man's mouth and he twitched for several seconds and then was still.

"You see?" Cleel said. "We got a bunch of murdcrin' Utes on the warpath, and by God, we're going to wipe them out!"

Davey's heart was pounding as he looked at the faces of the men gathered by the creek. They all had blood in their eyes, and if they listened to Cleel, he knew they'd all be dead in a month.

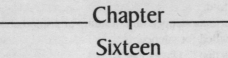

Chapter
Sixteen

Sheila heard the snap of a dry branch and the sound sent a chill shivering up her spine. She froze over the piece of wood she had been reaching for and hoped her galloping heart would settle down to a normal rhythm. She noticed that her outstretched hand was trembling. The fear rose up in her and she gasped for a breath through her suddenly dry mouth.

"Who's there?" she called out inanely, and listened only to the soft sound of the breeze in the scattered pines and junipers. Then she heard what sounded like a bird. But the melodic line was so pure, it sounded more like a flute. But who would play a flute out here, she wondered, and not a soul in sight?

The sound trailed off, and she thought after a moment that she must have imagined it. She bent down to pick up another dry branch, and then she heard other birdcalls from somewhere off in the small copse of trees. It was only an animal, she thought. Nothing to be afraid of. She looked up at the azure sky, toward the mountains. Small clouds floated serenely over the snowcapped peaks and she saw a hawk flying along the South Platte hunting for small game. It was such a peaceful scene, she thought. What could possibly mar the beauty of this place?

She continued to gather wood, hurrying now, and tried to quell the growing fear she felt at being all alone in such a desolate place. She had one bundle of firewood ready to carry back to the homestead and was nearly finished with another. She looked all around, but saw nothing out of the ordinary. Way off in the distance, she could make out some antelope feeding on the prairie, just the tops of their backs and their necks and pronghorns. A few birds flew in dark dots against the sky and the mountains, as always, were immutable, silent.

For a long time Sheila was able to gather her wood calmly. But when she was pulling the straps over her shoulders, preparing to bear the wood back to her home, she again heard the melodic sound. It was so crystal clear, and the notes so sustained, that she knew it either had to be coming from a bird she had never seen before . . . or from something else. A quirk of the wind? A flute? A hornpipe? She did not know.

Sheila usually enjoyed these times away from the Groots, but today was different. She knew that they had sent her off so they could talk about her, or plan something in secret. They had done this to her before. But today, Hans had seemed so serious. She wondered if it had anything to do with the trapper, Davey Longworth, or with that Arapaho, Eagle Heart. She had not been able to put either man out of her mind in the days since she had last seen them.

The fluting stopped, and Sheila was suddenly struck by a terrible sense of foreboding. Trying to shake off the feeling, she slung the bundles of wood over her back and shoulders, slipped the top strap across her forehead, adjusted the side straps on her shoulders, and tied the thong at her waist. She jiggled the bundles to see that they were secure and then started walking quickly back to the new house.

"Sun Hair."

She turned and saw something move in the copse of the trees. Her heart lodged in her throat like a lump of pudding.

"Me come," the man called out, and then she saw
an Indian step into view, resplendent in whitened elkskins,
bleached of all color, decorated with beads and porcupine
quills, a full headdress of perfectly matched eagle feathers,
with a wide strip of colored beads forming the headband. As
he walked toward her Sheila's legs began to quiver and she
felt a storm of wings in her stomach. She wanted to run, but
her feet seemed permanently fixed to the earth. She could
not speak. She could not move.

Then she saw that the Indian carried something in his
hands. She could not see what it was, but she was sure it
was a weapon of some kind. She was sure that the savage
was going to kill her or capture her.

Suddenly something flashed in the Indian's hands and
Sheila closed her eyes, prepared to die if that was to be her
fate. It seemed that her heart stopped as the footsteps drew
nearer. She wanted to cry out, but she knew it would be too
late and do little good. She knew that she did not have long
to live and held her breath as if to stop time in its tracks.

_____ Chapter _____
Seventeen

D avey stepped up to the group, Fritz following in his wake. Men were still talking even though John Cleel had called for quiet. The young trapper could see why. Three dead men lay in their midst, with two others severely wounded.

"I'd like to know what happened," Davey said, looking at one of the prospectors who had brought in the dead and wounded men.

"This ain't none of your business, mister," Cleel told him.

"Why not?" Davey asked.

"You ain't no prospector like the rest of us."

"Maybe not, but our bunch ran into Utes today, too."

"We know, but none of you got kilt."

"That ain't true," Peaches said. "We lost a man in the mountains, and Davey there watched old Caleb Wakefield die up at his digs."

"Well, I'm callin' the shots," Cleel returned.

"What I want to know," Davey continued, unperturbed, "is where the Utes jumped these boys."

"I'll tell him, John." A man stepped away from one of the dead men and spoke. "You're damned right I'll tell him."

"Go on ahead," Cleel invited, a sullen cast to his voice.

"Who are you?" Davey asked.

"Name's Lovell. Arnie Lovell."

"When did the Utes jump you?"

"Late this afternoon. About a dozen of 'em."

"Warn't that many, Arnie," a man called out from the crowd. "I counted eight."

" 'At's right, Jube," Arnie said. "Seemed like more. But we counted eight."

"You kill any?" Davey asked.

"Nary." The name of the man who spoke these words was Jubal Meek, but everyone called him Jube.

"Where were you when they attacked?" Davey asked. He was wondering if the Utes were the same bunch that had trapped them in the draw.

"South of here, 'bout three miles down the Platte."

"Don't tell him too damned much, Arnie," Jube cut in.

"That's close enough, mister," Arnie said. "We had some sluice boxes, a rocker or two, and some of us were panning."

"Find any color?" Davey asked.

"Maybe." Arnie looked away.

"That's none of your business, Longworth," Cleel said. "Now clear out and let us get back to ours."

"What's your play, Cleel?" Davey asked.

"I say we get up a war party of our own and go after them murderin' Utes and clean the whole nest out like a pack of rats."

"Hear! Hear!" some of the men shouted.

"There's plenty of us. I say we wipe 'em out before they kill any more prospectors. This land belongs to us as much as them."

Davey looked at the faces of the men gathered around Cleel. Their eyes flared with anger and some passed a jug around to give them courage, wiping their lips and waving their fists to show their support of John Cleel. He knew some of the men, the trappers, and they seemed to be in support of Cleel as well. Fritz stood nearby, his face devoid of expression, but Davey could not tell if he went along with the others or not.

These were rough men, Davey knew, and he had no doubt they would fight and not run. But he doubted many of them knew what they were facing. They were eager to follow any leader, especially a man who spoke their language, who knew what was in their hearts and minds. Cleel, he decided, was a hothead, and a fool if he thought he could lead a ragtag bunch such as this to victory.

"Are you with me?" Cleel shouted.

A cheer rose up from the men and Cleel grinned with the flush of success.

"We'll leave first thing in the morning," he went on. "We'll pick up their trail and follow 'em to their camp and kill every man jack of 'em."

"Hooray," shouted several men, and the rest joined in.

"Bring plenty of powder and ball. Check your rifles and pistols. We ride at dawn," Cleel said. "We'll get those murderin' bastards."

Another outburst from the gathering drowned out all other sound. Cleel stepped down from the stump and men slapped him on the back and grabbed his hand to shake it. Their murmurs died out as the men began to disperse.

"Cleel," Davey called, when he stepped away from the gladhanders. "A word with you."

"Either you're with us or agin' us, Longworth. I heard you was a damned Injun lover," Cleel said belligerently.

The men who were leaving stopped in their tracks and stared at Davey.

"Cleel, how many Utes you figure you'll find in that camp if you track to it?"

"I don't know. A couple dozen, maybe. Why? We got enough fighting men here to handle it."

"Have you been watching the hills the past few days?"

"Not particularly."

"Well, the Utes have been makin' smoke and flashing mirrors."

"So?"

"So they're callin' in all their bands, from the prairie and all through the Rockies."

"What are you gettin' at, Longworth?"

"Just this. If you attack that Ute camp, you'll stir up a hornet's nest. You'll be ass-deep in Utes before you even get out of their camp."

"So you say just let 'em be."

"For now. Until you know what they're up to."

"We know what they're up to. They've already killed, what? Four or five men."

"Cleel, you can't beat 'em. They figger the South Platte's a holy river and they don't want the white man to spoil it."

"We've got every right to use that river, same as them."

"They won't figger it that way, Cleel."

"I was right about you, Longworth. You're a damned Injun lover. The Utes have to be taken care of. And we aim to do it."

"If you do, Cleel, then even Cherry Creek won't be safe. They'll wipe out every white man in these parts."

"Not if we make the first move, they won't."

"Well, don't say I didn't warn you."

"Longworth, your advice ain't worth the breath it takes to say it."

Davey shrugged and turned to walk away. Fritz fell into step with him.

"Just stay the hell out of our way, Longworth," Cleel called out.

Davey ignored him and kept walking back toward the trader's camp.

"You made you an enemy there, Davey," Fritz observed.

"Likely," Davey said.

"I agree with you. Best to let sleeping dogs lie."

"Some good men will die. But the Utes are likely to go on the warpath anyway."

The two men arrived at the trader's camp. "I'll be seein' you, Fritz," Davey said. "I'm goin' to head out in the morning to pick up my caches."

"You watch your back, Davey. Cleel's a bad one."

"You watch yours, Fritz."

Davey took his horse and mules far enough up the creek so that he could hear anyone approaching. He made a dry camp and a false camp. He didn't know Creel, or what he might do, but the man was a hothead and could be counted on to do anything to maintain his place as leader of the prospectors.

He hoped he would not have a run-in with Cleel, but he expected that they might tangle one day. When he crawled into his bedroll, he looked up at the night sky, the sparkling stars scattered across the heavens like diamonds.

And before he fell asleep, he thought of Sheila.

Chapter
Eighteen

Sheila opened her eyes and the apparition was still there.
"Please don't hurt me," she murmured as the elk-skin-clad Indian drew closer.

"No hurt," the Indian said. "Friend."

"Eagles Heart?" she asked, recognizing the brave.

"Yes, me Eagle Heart," the Arapaho said, his speech heavily accented, then held out the bundle in his hands. "Me come. Wan to show Sun Hair."

Sheila's heart still raced and she felt the heat of her fear and apprehension on her face. She slipped out of the straps that held the wood ricks in place and let them settle to the ground. There was no place to run, she knew, but she wondered what Eagle Heart would do. She had never been alone with a man since she had reached maturity and it was unsettling to have such a fearsome presence come so close.

"D-don't hurt me," she said.

"No, not hurt."

Eagle Heart stopped a few feet from her, took some deep breaths, and patted his chest. "You," he said.

It took her a minute or two to realize that he was trying to calm her down, that he wanted her to take deep breaths, too. She smiled weakly and began to breathe long and deep. She felt immediately calmer.

"Good," Eagle Heart said.

"I—I feel better. Do you speak English?"

"Speak little. Speak good."

"Yes," she said, relieved. She wanted to giggle with gratitude that he had not attacked her. Yet she was still trembling.

Eagle Heart came still closer, then stooped down and placed the bundle he carried in his hands on the ground.

"Come," he said. "Look."

Fascinated, Sheila stepped closer and bent over to see what was in the bundle. Eagle Heart unfolded the outer layer, a swatch of buckskin, exposing a beautiful cape of ermine skins, white as snow. This, too, he unfolded, and there, in the center, lay a small pouch of whitened elkskin covered with beads and tack heads and a ripple of porcupine quills.

"For Sun Hair," he announced proudly.

"For me? What is it?"

"Take," he said.

Sheila picked up the pouch. The drawstring was made from a leather thong that was pulled tight so that the opening was puckered shut. Eagle Heart signed with his hands that she should open it. She tugged on the thong, working it open.

"Look," Eagle Heart said.

Sheila peered inside, but it was too dark to see anything. But she knew there were objects inside. She reached in and pulled out some beads, and a gold nugget. She gasped, held it up to the light.

"Shining stone," Eagle Heart said. "Yellow like sun."

"Yes," she breathed. "It's gold."

Eagle Heart reached over, touched the small bag with his finger. "Medicine pouch. Good medicine."

"Thank you," Sheila said. She fingered the beads. They were very beautiful; yellow, red, and blue.

"You keep," Eagle Heart said. "Good medicine."

"Yes." Sheila attempted a smile. "Beautiful. Very pretty."

She put the objects back in the pouch, drew the draw-string tight. She clutched the medicine bag to her chest, then thanked Eagle Heart again.

"I—I must go," she said.

"Wood." Eagle Heart pointed to the ricks on the ground.

"Yes."

"Need horse."

Sheila laughed, nodding. While Eagle Heart did not know many words, she felt that he was an understanding man, that they could converse on another level than her conversations with the Groots. She was surprised that she no longer feared him. His gift had touched her heart. She must find a way to hide it from the Groots. The medicine pouch was something special. She did not know the significance of it, what it meant to Eagle Heart and the Arapahos, but she sensed that it was very important, more than just a keepsake.

It was then that Sheila saw the flute lying at one edge of the ermine skins. She smiled, and Eagle Heart picked it up, handed it to her. She rolled it between her fingers. It was a delicate instrument, decorated with designs she had never seen before, but the etchings resembled scrimshaw drawings she had seen in St. Louis when she was a girl. She handed the flute back to Eagle Heart. He set it back on the hides and began to move his hands, speaking in broken English. He brought his right hand up to his heart and made a small circle.

"Eagle Heart like Sun Hair. Big heart for Sun Hair."

"I—I like you, too, Eagle Heart."

"Me come see. Bring pony. Bring present. Give to father for Sun Hair. Take Sun Hair to lodge. Make happy."

Sheila's face turned a rosy hue as her blood ran hot. She knew what the Indian was saying, and his simple words and the signs he made touched her deeply.

"Groot," she said. "Not father."

"You slave girl."

Sheila started to shake her head in reply, but thought better of it. Perhaps she could not make the Arapaho brave understand. So she nodded and bowed her head.

"Eagle Heart buy. Take to lodge. No be slave girl. Groot bad heart."

"Groot will not sell me," she said.

"Groot take presents. Sell"—he searched for the word—"you."

"No, he will not do this."

Eagle Heart's face clouded with his fierce scowl. "Me take," he said. "Make Sun Hair wife."

Again Sheila's face flushed, and she didn't know what to say. She was flattered, but she knew she could not live in Eagle Heart's world. Their lives were so different. But she sensed that he would not understand her reasoning and she didn't want to hurt his feelings.

"Don't come," she implored. "Please."

"Me come," Eagle Heart said, and then folded his ermine and rewrapped the bundle. He stood to full height and smiled a crooked smile. "Heart big," he announced, tapping his chest.

Sheila shook her head, but did not say the words again. She knew she could not stop Eagle Heart from doing what he wanted to do, doing what was in his heart.

The Arapaho made the sign of good-bye. Sheila imitated it, knowing at that moment that she wanted to learn Eagle Heart's language, both the spoken word and the hand signs.

"Good-bye," she said. Then she picked up the straps and the bundles of firewood. She harnessed herself with the leather straps and turned to walk away.

"Me come soon," Eagle Heart promised.

Sheila turned to tell him once again that she did not want him to come, but she couldn't speak. She knew that she wanted to see the Arapaho again, even though she had no doubt that Hans would be angry.

She nodded and saw a faint smile appear on Eagle Heart's face.

She turned and walked back toward home. When she turned around, Eagle Heart had disappeared. But she thought she heard the sound of his flute and the melody stayed in her mind as she trudged under the heavy load of wood. She was light-headed and happy as she felt the medicine pouch tucked behind her waistband. She stopped for a moment. She blushed, then began walking again. She chided herself for what she was thinking, for wondering if the men of the Arapaho tribe kissed their women.

Chapter Nineteen

Three shapes emerged from the deep shadows. They presented no discernible images as they crept toward Davey's false camp. He heard the pad of footfalls and saw the shadows glide across the narrow opening in the trees. They might have been human or animal, he could not tell.

But Davey slid his rifle and pistol from beneath his blanket and slowly sat up. His silhouette was masked by the tree behind him, he knew. He carefully swung his rifle around and put his index finger inside the trigger guard. Then he cocked the hammer as he squeezed gently on the trigger so that the click of the sear engaging could not be heard. He brought the hammer to full cock and leaned back against the tree to wait.

The shadows stopped moving for a moment, then broke farther apart and surrounded his false figure in the blanket, a rock for his neck, dead branches representing his body underneath the covering.

The three men started viciously beating the blanket. Davey heard the crunch of the branches as they broke and the snap of staves striking the rock. Then one of the men pulled out a pistol, which gleamed faintly in the moonlight, and fired a shot into the tangle of blanket, limbs, and stones. Orange sparks flew from the barrel of the pistol and he heard the crack of the explosion, the thud of the bullet into the earth.

Still, Davey did not fire. He had only a brief glimpse of the men when the pistol fired, but he could not see their faces, make out who they were. One of the men cursed as he kicked the blanket. Wood clattered and rang off stone and the blanket settled into a formless heap a few feet away.

"He ain't here," said one man.

"Smart sombitch, ain't he?" asked another.

"We'd better get the hell out of here. He's probably watchin' us."

Davey recognized the latter voice. It belonged to the man who had fired the pistol, tried to kill him in his sleep.

"Peaches," Davey whispered silently.

The men ran away from the false camp and Davey eased the hammer back down on his rifle. He could easily have shot Peaches and maybe gotten another with his pistol, but then he'd have to answer a lot of questions.

He was surprised that Peaches had wanted to kill him. As far as Davey knew, he had no quarrel with the man. But he smelled whiskey in the air after the men left and decided that Cleel had persuaded some of the free trappers to throw in with him on his Ute-killing expedition.

Davey wanted no part of that senselessness. Just as he had warned, Cleel would be stirring up a hornet's nest. No white man would be safe on the plains or in the mountains if the Utes gathered forces and went on the warpath. There would be blood on the ground and fresh scalps hanging in the Ute lodges.

He knew he had to warn the Groots. He would do that on his way back to pick up his caches. One thing was for certain: there would be no more sleep for him this night. Those men who had tried to kill him would go back to their camp and keep on drinking until they got up enough courage to try again.

Making little noise, Davey packed up his belongings, saddled his horse, and tied the empty panniers to the mules' backs. He would have to live off the land and go without staples awhile longer. Well, he thought, he could do that.

He rode slowly up the creek and crossed at a shallow spot and then headed northwest, judging his direction by the North Star. His belly growled with hunger and he wished he had a cup of coffee to keep him awake, warm his innards. It was cold under the clear, starry sky and he shook out his capote and wrapped the belt tight around his waist.

He rode on toward the South Platte, listening to the soft sigh of the wind on the budding grasses. The cool breeze on his face kept him awake.

He wondered while he rode which side Fritz would be on when the prospectors gathered at dawn to search out the Utes. He wondered if his former partner knew that Peaches and two other men had tried to put out his, Davey's, lamp.

Davey smiled. He was lucky, he guessed. If he hadn't learned that old Indian trick of making a false camp, he might be dead now. The white man, he thought, could learn a lot from his red-skinned brothers if he only took a little time to make a friend or two, instead of thinking of the Indians as savages.

Too late for men like Cleel, though, he thought. Maybe too late for all those men back on Cherry Creek. When he and the others had that run-in with the Utes below Lookout Mountain, possibly none of the others had realized how close they had come to being wiped out.

Now, Davey was convinced that the Utes broke off the attack not out of fear, but because they had already demonstrated that they could win the fight with only a small number of warriors. For days now, their warriors had been signaling to their brothers to come to the mountains and gather for a big powwow. Those prospectors on Cherry Creek did not know what they would encounter in the Ute camp.

Davey was sure that if the white men attacked the camp, they would not find a mere dozen or so warriors, but an entire tribe of seasoned fighters. The Utes did not camp near noisy streams, but on high ground, well away from water. Long before the whites reached the Ute camp, the tribe would know they were going to be attacked.

And they would be waiting.

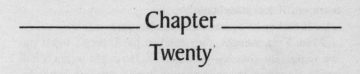

Chapter Twenty

Fritz Stamm rubbed the sand of sleep from his eyes and sat up in his blankets. He had finished up his business with Bill Gwaltney the night before and had gone to bed early. His sleep had been disturbed by men coming and going in camp, and loud talking, but he had finally drifted off. Now it was quiet, quiet enough for him to overhear a nearby conversation.

"Why didn't you go back and try again?" someone was saying. Fritz recognized the voice as John Cleel's.

"A man like that won't give you a second chance."

Peaches, Fritz thought. And another man spoke up just then.

"He was awatchin' us, sure as turds float." A prospector named McGuinn. Fritz knew who he was. A backstabber from New Orleans, keelboatman, thief, once a trapper up on the Ohio who stole furs rather than trade or trap for them. A cutthroat.

"He had us cold," said another man. "I could smell him in the dark." Fritz did not recognize this voice. Who in hell were they talking about? He shoved the blankets aside and stood up slowly. The men were still talking.

"Is he still here?" Cleel asked.

"How the hell should we know?" Peaches again. "Davey's his own man. He keeps to himself."

"Well, I don't want him in our hair when we go out this morning," Cleel stated coldly.

"I reckon he's gone on," Peaches said.

So, Fritz thought, they tried to put Davey's lights out last night. The treacherous bastards. He ought to put a ball in Cleel's gullet. Peaches, though, was a surprise. What did he have against Davey? Jealousy perhaps.

Fritz thought back to the winter in the mountains. Tried to remember what Peaches had said, if he had talked about Davey much. Well, he had asked some questions. Not a lot, but some. Fritz tried to remember the words Peaches had used.

"How come you don't trap no more with that feller Davey?" Peaches had asked shortly after they had gone up into the mountains, before the first snow.

"He has his ways, I got mine," Fritz had replied.

"What ways?"

"Davey can worry a man."

"How's that?"

"He goes off by hisself a lot and don't talk much when he gets back."

"Where does he go?" Peaches wanted to know.

"I seen him making talk and smoke with the Arapahos," Fritz told him.

Things like that. Probably he should have kept his mouth shut. Davey was never any trouble, but he'd be gone from camp for days, and when he came back, he always had new moccasins, prime pelts, gewgaws and what-nots made by the Indians.

Sometimes he'd hear Davey talking in his sleep, but it warn't no English, it was some foreign tongue, and not German ner French neither. Probably Injun, Fritz decided, but he'd never mention it to Davey. But sometimes that sleep talk would make Fritz's hair stand on end.

Another time Peaches wanted to know if Davey had gotten him a squaw when they were trapping together.

"I don't know," Fritz had replied.

"Some say he has him a blanket woman, a sleeping dictionary," Peaches had said.

"Well, I never seen none."

"He might even have him a kid."

"Well, he never said such," Fritz had said, and the subject was dropped real quick.

Maybe that's how word got around that Davey was an Indian lover. Fritz didn't know, but the fat was in the fire now and there would be hell to pay.

Fritz grabbed up his rifle, stuck his pistol in his belt, and walked up the creek. Dawn still held the land in its grip, with fog on the water and in the trees, and a brisk chill breeze was blowing down from the mountains. At one or two of the camps, the men were awake and stirring the coals for cookfires. He smelled meat cooking from somewhere, meat and grease and lard and bannock, the smells all mingled in the air. They made him hungry. When he smelled coffee cooking, his stomach twisted and he started salivating. But he would not break off from his mission.

Fritz found the place where Davey had slept, and the false camp. He knelt down and dug into the dirt beneath the sticks until he found a spent lead ball. Not that he needed any proof, but it felt good to confirm his suspicions after what he had heard earlier.

He glanced toward the place where Davey had actually spent some of the night. He measured the distance mentally. There was no doubt in Fritz's mind that Davey had the drop on his would-be assassins. He could have killed one or more of them before they knew what hit them.

So Davey had lit a shuck and was gone. Probably to return in a few days with the furs from his cache. Fritz hoped he would see the young man again, but one way or the other, he knew there was big trouble ahead. Cleel was set on wip-ing out the Utes and Davey was against any such attack. Fritz didn't know if Cleel could do what he set out to do, but he hoped Davey was wrong. Maybe the Utes did need to be taught a lesson. Certainly all their lives were in danger if the Utes gathered strength and went on the warpath.

As he turned to leave Davey's campsite Fritz heard a rifle shot, then shouting. He walked slowly back down the creek and saw men dressing for war, checking their ri-fles, gathering powder and ball, slinging on their possibles pouches, and saddling their horses. When he returned to his bed ground, Cleel was giving instructions.

"We'll pick up the trail of those murderin' Utes," he was saying, "and follow them right into their damned camp. Kill 'em all, man, woman, and child. No mercy."

His words were greeted with shouts from the assem-bled prospectors and those trappers who meant to follow the warlike Cleel.

"Mount up, and make sure you've got plenty of pow-der and ball. Keep your powder dry and follow my lead."

With that, Cleel walked to his horse and climbed into the saddle. Others did the same, and the clatter and creak of leather and rattle of pistols and muskets and mountain rifles filled the air.

"Ain't you comin', Fritz?" Peaches asked as the hop-per rode by.

Fritz shook his head.

"I'll bring you a Ute scalp." Peaches laughed.

"Just bring your own damned scalp back," Fritz said, but his heart wasn't in it. Peaches had tried to kill Davey dur-ing the night and Fritz knew he could never trust him again.

Tall Tom was going, too, he noticed, and he waved at Fritz, grinned wide. Then he let out a war whoop and the oth-ers picked it up, and as the column of men rode away from Cherry Creek, they sounded more like Indians than white men.

Fritz wondered if he'd ever see any of them again.

When the camp was quiet, there were only a few hard-bitten trappers left, and Bill Gwaltney, who walked up to Fritz.

"Well, they're gone," he said.

"I reckon. You don't side with Cleel?"

"He's a snake. Men like that live on other people's courage. He has none for himself," Gwaltney said grimly.

"He seems pretty much on top of things."

"When they get into a fight, John will hold back, and if the battle turns against him, he'll be the first to ride back with his tail tucked 'twixt his legs."

"I reckon they have a chance."

"Maybe, but look." Gwaltney pointed to the mountains, still smoky in the morning haze. There were balls of smoke rising at intervals from several different points. The two men watched mirrors flash in the foothills.

"The Utes already know he's coming," Gwaltney said.

Fritz sighed. He knew it was true. And he wondered if Cleel was stone blind with ambition. Surely he must see that smoke and the mirror flashes. He must know that he was leading his men into a wilderness that was like a fortress to the Utes.

"I don't reckon they'll be comin' back," Fritz said.

"Oh, some of them will, Fritz. You'll damned sure see John Cleel again. But there'll be a lot of blood spilled and this may mark the end of the white man in this part of Jefferson Territory."

"It's that damned South Platte River," Fritz said. "The Utes say it's theirs, and the prospectors think it's flowing with gold."

Gwaltney said nothing. He and Fritz watched the smoke signals and kept their thoughts to themselves as the sun rose over the horizon in the east and the creek shimmered golden in the early light.

Chapter
Twenty-One

D avey rode for three days toward the Cache de la Poudre, sleeping fitfully off the trail, always on high ground, always in a dry camp so that he made no fires. The smoke signals and the mirror flashes stopped at the close of the first day, and again at noon on the second. He was pushing his horse and his mules, he knew, but the signaling seemed ominous and even more threatening during the intervals when they stopped.

Davey figured that it must have taken Cleel and his bunch two days to reach the Ute camp, at least. Three maybe. Time enough for the scattered tribes and braves to bunch up and wait. So maybe on the third day Cleel attacked. If the Utes let him get as far as their camp. And maybe the whites and Utes fought for a day or more. . . . Then what? Davey could not predict the outcome, but he noticed that there were no smoke or mirror signals on the morning of the fourth day when he reached the South Platte and so he figured maybe Cleel might have done just what he set out to do.

Could he and his band have defeated the Utes? Davey thought it unlikely. The Utes were at home in the mountains and the whites were not. The white men would be gasping for breath and would tire easily at the high altitude. The Utes were used to the thin air and would not be easily overcome.

The morning was chill. It was still winter in some places high in the Rockies and the cold air blew down onto the plain from the snow-flocked peaks. He shivered in his jacket and almost missed seeing the smoke rising in the air ahead of him. Right where the Groot place ought to be.

Davey quickened his pace. He had news for the settlers, and a warning, and he was anxious to see Sheila Stewart again, find out more about her. The lazy spiral of smoke told him the Groots had a fire going, or at least he hoped so. Too soon for the Utes to attack the settlers, he thought. But if Cleel had stirred them up and not accounted himself well, the Indians would swarm down onto the prairie like maddened wasps.

The mules were heaving when Davey hove up over the hill and saw the Groot house. It had grown since he had last been there. It was fully roofed, and as he drew closer he saw that it was chinked in and looked like a small fort, with a lookout tower and gun ports on the walls. Groot and his family had done a good job. It wouldn't mean a damned thing if hostile Indians attacked in large numbers, but it was better than living out of a wagon or in a tent.

Davey watched the trail carefully for tracks, and was not surprised to see that there were signs of a large number of ponies, and drag marks from heavily laden travois. The tracks all headed north, and he knew that the Arapahos had returned from Santa Fe for the summer hunt.

As he approached the Groot house he saw that the main body of tracks did not stop; scouts had evidently looked at the "fort" and ridden around it, but then had gone on. He wondered if Groot had traded with them.

His heart sank as he saw no signs of activity at the house. It was very quiet. He rode around the wooden structure slowly, but saw no signs that an attack had taken place.

"Hello, Hans Groot," Davey called as he came around to the front entrance.

A face appeared at one of the windows. He saw the sun glint off a shock of blond hair.

"Sheila?"

"They are not here," Sheila said. "They are working in the field."

"Are you all right?" he asked. Sheila's head was dipped, so that he could not see her face.

"You'd best ride on," she said.

"I want to talk to you first," Davey told her.

"Please. I—I can't."

"Don't argue with me, Sheila. Come out of there now or I'm coming in."

Davey swung down from his horse, tied the animals up to a support rail on the porch.

"I'll come out. But only for a minute. Then you must go."

Davey said nothing, but Sheila's face disappeared from the window and he heard her footsteps on the flooring. A moment later she stood just outside the door.

"This is as far as I will come," she said.

"Sheila, what's the matter?" She was still trying to hide her face. "Let me take a look at you."

"No," she said, with firm emphasis.

"Something's wrong."

"No, it—it's all right. I'm fine."

"Like hell you are." He took the steps two at a time and stood in front of her. He chucked her under the chin and tilted her head up.

Davey sucked in a breath. "What happened to you?" he asked. Sheila's face was blotched and bruised. There was a dark purple half-moon shadow under one of her eyes. Her jaw was slightly swollen, and her lips were puffed and cracked.

Sheila jerked her head away and lowered it again. She began to cry, and Davey held her shoulders in a tight grip until her trembling stopped.

"Who did this to you?" he asked. Then he looked at her arms and wrists. There were bruises on them, too.

"Don't pay it no mind," she said.

"You've been badly beaten, Sheila. I can't ignore what they did to you."

"Please, Mr. Longworth."

"Davey."

"Davey."

"I want the truth, Sheila. You tell me, or I'll beat it out of them."

"Then will you go, Davey?"

"Then I'll decide what to do."

"It'll be worse if I tell you."

"Dammit, I already know you were beaten. I just want to know why and who did it. Was it Maddy?"

Sheila nodded.

"Hans, too?"

"Y-yes," she stammered.

"What about the boy, Kris?"

"He—he held me while Maddy and Hans beat me."

Davey stifled a curse. "Why?"

Sheila did not say anything for several seconds. Then she looked up at Davey, her blue-flame eyes burning into his. She took a deep breath and put her hands on his arms, holding him tightly, as if to pull courage from the feel of him.

She told him about her meeting with Eagle Heart while she was out gathering wood. She told him about the flute and the medicine pouch, how she had hidden it in her clothing.

"When I returned with the wood, the Groots all looked at me funny," she recounted. "They wanted to know why I had taken so long."

"And what did you tell them?"

"What I always tell them. That it's getting harder and harder to find wood on this side of the river. I told Hans that he should build a raft so that I could find wood in the foothills."

"What did he say?"

"He said that I just wanted a raft so that I could escape down the South Platte."

"Is that why you wanted one?"

"I—I never thought about such a thing. I told Hans the truth."

"Did he believe you?" Davey asked. Sheila still clung fast to him, her fingers digging into the flesh of his arms.

"No. He called me a liar and then he slapped me. I tried to get away and then Maddy said they had something to tell me."

"What was that?"

"She said that they had decided that I was going to marry Kris."

"What? Do you love him?"

"No, I hate him. I told Maddy that, and she slapped me. I ran out of the house and down to the river. I wanted to dive in and drown myself."

"You poor girl." Davey shook his head sadly.

"Before I could do anything, Kris came after me and dragged me back. That night they tied me to my bed, and every night they do this."

"That's wrong," Davey said. "Very wrong."

"They watch me all the time. Until today."

"What happened today?"

"They found the medicine pouch. That is, Maddy did, and she asked me what it was. I told her I found it while I was gathering wood."

"And she didn't believe you," Davey said. It was not a question.

"No. She said it looked new. She grabbed my arm and took me into the kitchen, where Hans and Kris were having breakfast. She threw the pouch on the table and accused me of sneaking off to see Eagle Heart."

"And then?"

"Kris held me while Maddy and Hans slapped and hit me. They said if I ever thought about running away or seeing Eagle Heart again, they would kill me."

"That's serious," Davey said. "A most serious threat."

"I know."

"Why did they leave you alone, then?"

"They said they wanted me to just try and run away. That would give them the excuse they needed to come after me and kill me. They said they'd check on me every hour or so and I'd better be here."

"When were they last here?"

"About twenty minutes ago. Not all of them. Just Kris. He said he couldn't wait until we got married. He told me they were going to take me to one of the Dutch preachers in a month. Davey, I'm terrified of Kris. He's tried to rape me and now I'm going to be forced to marry him."

"Well, we'll see about that. Sheila, even if you are bonded to them, they have no right to beat you, and certainly no right to tie you up at night. I'm going to get to the bottom of this. Do you know how long your servitude was to last?"

"My mother told me I was to be bonded for five years and then I would be returned to her."

"You've been with the Groots for more than six years now."

"I know. I thought there must be some mistake. But I asked Maddy about it one day, and she said I was bonded to them forever."

"Forever?"

"That's what she said."

"She lied to you, Sheila. You're no more a bondservant than I am."

"I can't prove it," she said.

"You may not have to. I'm going to get you out of here while I figure out what to do. The legal thing."

"They'll never agree to that."

Davey's mind raced. He didn't want to break the law. Maybe the Groots had bought Sheila outright, but he didn't think that was legal. No, there was something they were holding back from her and he had to find out the truth.

Sheila released her grip on Davey's arm. She dabbed at the tears streaking her face. Davey helped her wipe them, using his sleeve to gently brush away the tracks.

"Get your things together, Sheila," he told her.

"What are you going to do?" she asked.

Davey stepped outside. In the distance he glimpsed Hans, Maddy, and Kris heading toward the house. They carried rakes and hoes and Hans had a rifle over his shoulder.

"Here they come," Sheila said, her voice quaking with fear. Again she asked, "What are you going to do, Davey?"

"You'll see," was Davey's only reply. "Just get your things."

He walked down the porch steps and stepped to his horse. He drew his rifle from its sheath and stood there waiting for the Groots.

Chapter
Twenty-Two

Cleel and his followers found the place where the prospectors were attacked and plenty of fresh tracks that the Utes had made. Peaches was a good tracker and he led them along the route the Utes had taken. Two men rode with him, acting as scouts, ranging ahead and alongside the trail.

The Utes had made no attempt to throw off any pursuers. Instead, they rode straight for the mountains, following an old game trail. At the first high ridge they turned right, still following an old trail, and there they joined up with another band. Peaches figured the Indians numbered about two dozen now. It was hard to count the tracks, but he figured at least twenty or so braves were in a bunch.

The trappers and prospectors camped that night deep in the woods. Cleel oversaw the billets, putting some of his men in a clump of spruce, others amid the pines, and some near the juniper and fir trees. He set military watches, four hours each, four men to a watch. There was a lot of grumbling from the men, who were not used to riding a horse at a high altitude, but John Cleel managed to put them at ease.

"This is necessary," he told them. "If we don't take care of the Ute problem, we'll never be able to become rich men. And that's why we came out here to this godforsaken place, isn't it?"

In the face of this unassailable logic, the grumbling died down and Cleel put himself on the first watch. They passed the night without incident, although one man on the morning watch said that he had seen some shadows moving and thought they might be Indians.

But no fresh tracks were found the next day, although Peaches swore that there were places that looked as if the earth had been swept with a broom. The pony tracks of the Utes crisscrossed creeks and small streams, and for a time the trail was lost. The small army of white men came upon rocks jutting out of the mountainside and large tracts of thick pines, where the ground was littered with deadfallen trees they had to go around or walk over, leading their horses through the thick graveyard of ponderous trees. There was a hush to the forest that made the men nervous and Cleel kept the scouts in close lest they lose sight of one another in the thickness of the somber glades.

They came upon bear scat and heard a mountain lion cough, and the crows screamed their passage up the mountain. Cleel cursed them and told the men to be quiet, but they made a lot of noise and scared up elk on their beds and jumped mule deer out of the thickets.

The trail wound around a mountain and then doubled back to another high hill and over that and into a steep canyon that was hell on horses and men. Clouds of insects jumped the party and ragged at them until another altitude was achieved; then the mood of the men blackened like the shadows in the thickest parts of the deep forest and they began to curse among themselves. The clouds shadowed the sun and made the terrain even darker, so that it was like night though the sun stood high in the blue sky.

Peaches followed the tracks along a narrow ridge and onto a higher place where the trail narrowed even more in the rimrock. He saw a cougar leave its shallow cave and bound downward through the trees until it disappeared into the deep silence.

It was at the end of the third day that the Ute tracks disappeared along a steep rocky slope and Cleel halted the men and gave them his thoughts. All along the way they had blazed their trail, hacking large square wounds in lofty pines so that they could find their way back to Cherry Creek, and now he had to make a decision. He called in Peaches and the scouts and they all formed a circle in the open air that was so thin, the men had headaches and gasped for breath.

"Men, this is tough going," Cleel began. "We've come a long way and haven't found the Ute camp."

"We ought to go back," said a man named Richard Wales. "They done buffaloed us."

"We can go back," Cleel agreed, "but I feel we're close to their camp. This is the kind of place where the Utes would go. It's high up and hard to get to. Now, if we go over this next promontory, I just bet they'll be camped on the next high place."

"Sounds right to me," Peaches confirmed. He reached in his pocket and dug out some objects, which he held out in his hand. "I been pickin' these arrerheads up the last hunnert yards. Look around you, they're thick as fleas."

"Arrowheads?" Tall Tom asked. "How do you know they're Utes'?"

"Look at 'em. They're black as coal. Obsidian. Utes like 'em better'n flint."

The men passed the obsidian arrowheads around and marveled at their glistening and their sharpness.

"Spooky," said Wales.

"Well, them arrerheads mean there's Utes close by, like they threw the bad ones away, maybe off'n them rocks up yonder."

The men looked up and pictured Ute braves tossing the

culls over the cliff, and they stirred uneasy and fingered their rifle locks.

"See?" Cleel said. "We're close, damned close, and I say we go on one or two more cliffs, and by damn I bet we come on them Utes lolling about and braggin' at what they done to us."

Cleel was a powerful talker and a good persuader, because the men got a second wind and voted to go on awhile longer. That was when Cleel made his first bad decision.

"Here's what we'll do," he began. "We'll split up, half and half and encircle that cliff above us. If they're up there, we'll have 'em flanked on two sides. If not, we'll gather again and reconnoiter. Then we'll do the same thing for the next chunk of higher ground."

"Sounds good to me," one man said.

"Let's do 'er," Tall Tom said.

"Walk your horses and don't make no noise," Cleel told them. "Now let's go get 'em."

Peaches led the group flanking to the left and Cleel headed off with the rest on the right. The two groups encircled the bluff, leading their horses over broken talus and craggy remnants of ancient landslides. The climb was steep and the men puffed at the lack of oxygen.

Rocks clattered as men and horses climbed the steep slope to the plateau above. Peaches crawled the last few yards so that he would not present an easy target. He motioned for the others to stay behind while he slowly made his way over the rugged ground, his rifle ready in his right hand.

He peered over the top of the ledge and saw no sign of any Indian. Then he waited until he saw someone peek over the right side of the ledge. He waved and Cleel waved back. Immediately Peaches beckoned to the others to climb up to the top. He stood up and looked all around.

There was an ominous silence around all the white men now standing on the plateau. Some picked up chipped arrowheads and pieces of knives that had broken in the process of sharpening. There were signs that the Utes had camped at this spot in recent history, but not in the past several days or months.

"Plenty of pony tracks," Cleel said to Peaches.

"They come through here all right. But it's an old camp, still cold from winter."

"How long ago?" Cleel asked.

"Maybe a day, half a day," Peaches said.

"Then they can't be far away."

"Maybe, maybe not." Peaches looked up at the next plateau that he knew to be there, above the next ridge of rimrock. "They could be right above us. Or they could have gone on."

"We'll have to risk it," Cleel said. "To get this close and turn back . . ."

"I reckon we'll come acrost 'em pretty soon," Tall Tom put in. "I can smell 'em."

Peaches, as if to test Tall Tom's supposition, sniffed the air. All he could smell was pine and balsam.

"Well, let's split up again," Cleel said. "We'll take the right flank; Peaches you take the left."

"Watch yore topknot," Peaches warned, a leering grin wrinkling his face.

Cleel sent Tall Tom up around the precipice first while he held back and split his men up again into two groups, scattering them along the slope and then sending them up to the next plateau.

Peaches spread his men out, too, and they climbed the slope together at his signal. Rocks tumbled down as the men clawed their way to the top and slithered over the rimrock like lizards. Just as Peaches and Cleel's men reached the ledge, a great stillness seemed to descend on the mountains, as if the wind was taking a breath, and then the air filled with a soft whooshing sound. Peaches turned and saw black lines against the horizon, like iron filings on a magnetized surface. They seemed to float through the air in slow motion, but he knew what they were.

Then one of the men suddenly cried out as an obsidian-tipped arrow struck him in the back. He fell backward and his horse spooked and turned around, plunging back down the slope.

Cleel cried out a warning as his men were attacked. Arrows struck with unerring accuracy and men began rolling and falling down the talus-slick slope, creating miniature landslides. Men screamed and fired their rifles into the air.

There were no Ute targets. Arrows seemed to fly out of nowhere, not only from behind, but now from above as well. The men on both sides of the plateau milled around, dug into the ground for cover as arrows whirred overhead and thudded into living flesh or caromed off rocks.

"For God's sake, get us off this mountain," a man cried, and then threw up his arms as an arrow pierced his gullet.

Cleel ran down the slope off to his right, leading his horse as arrows kicked up dust around him. Tall Tom followed his lead, mounting his horse when he hit the fringe of the trees. More men followed suit. Peaches rallied his men to keep on going and they dragged their horses up the slope like sledges, then mounted at Peaches' command and rode into the timber, arrows whistling among them like the sound of keening ghosts.

Moments later the Utes burst from their cover atop sturdy, full-chested ponies. They fell upon the wounded men caught on the rimrock and began striking coup and taking scalps. Their war cries sent a chilling message to the fleeing men who raced their horses down through the timber at breakneck speed.

When Peaches looked back, he saw no Utes in retreat, and after a time he was alone. Occasionally he heard a horse crash through the timber, and once he caught the sound of a man crying out for help, but there was no way to determine where he was.

He wondered if Cleel had escaped alive. And he wondered if Tall Tom had made it. He remembered seeing the Utes emerge from the woods and ride up the treacherous slope as if they were charging across flat ground, their bows nocked with arrows, the strings drawn tight.

He knew that many of the white men had been killed. He also knew that Cleel was going to have a lot of explaining to do. "Damn," he said aloud, and then cursed himself for making noise.

Now there'd be hell to pay. Davey had been right. The Utes were the victors and now they would run every white man in Jefferson Territory out of the country, or leave their blood and bones to feed the prairie grasses.

Chapter Twenty-Three

Sheila, trembling, started to go back into the house as the Groot family plodded toward her and Davey from the field. "Don't make it any worse for me, Davey, please," she said.

"We've got to have this out, Sheila, once and for all."

"You're not going to shoot them, are you?" She glanced at his rifle.

"No, not unless Hans shoots first. You stay right where you are."

Reluctantly, Sheila clung to the doorjamb, her face drained of color, visibly shaking. Davey had never seen another human being so terrified. He had seen men die, seen women die, too, but none had showed such fear. Sheila wasn't afraid of much, he figured, but when it was three against one, and your every move was watched, and you faced beatings almost every day, then you had good reason to be fearful. He had no doubt that if he rode away, minded his own business, the Groots would promptly beat Sheila within an inch of her life just for talking to him.

"You there," yelled Hans when he was within earshot. "I told you not to come around here."

"Well, I'm here, Groot, and you're going to have to bear up under it."

"What do you say? I shoot you where you stand, Longworth."

Groot began to bring his rifle up to his shoulder.

Davey had his rifle at his hip, already aimed at Hans before the man's rifle butt lifted past his belly.

"You touch that trigger, Groot, and you're a dead man."

Kris raised a hoe over his head and started running toward Davey, but Maddy jumped forward and grabbed her son before he could take three steps. Hans lowered his rifle.

"What do you want?" he demanded.

"A serious talk, for one thing," Davey replied.

"We have nothing to talk about," Hans said, his accent thick. "We mind our own business. You mind yours."

Davey stood his ground until the three walked up to him. Then he lowered the barrel of his rifle, put one hand on the butt of his .60-caliber smoothbore pistol. It was not a threatening move, but it told Hans that he was ready to fight at close quarters.

Maddy looked up at Sheila, who still stood in the doorway. But the girl was no longer quaking in fear. Instead, she seemed to have summoned up some hidden resolve.

"State your business, then, Longworth, and then be gone from here. You are trespassing."

Davey waited a moment before responding. He looked into Hans's eyes, then looked hard at Maddy, who quickly dipped her head, breaking eye contact. Lastly, he stared at Kris, who wore a defiant look on his face, with his jaw set tight and his lips clamped firmly in a Teutonic frown.

"You're quite a bunch." Davey shook his head in disgust. "The three of you picking on a poor defenseless girl." He cocked a thumb in Sheila's direction. "A girl who has done no harm to you, but works for you without pay. Drudge work at that."

"That is our business, I have told you over and over," Hans said.

"That's right, mister," Maddy put in belligerently, but sidled closer to her husband as she spoke. "We only punish Sheila when she has been bad."

"I know what you do to her, Mrs. Groot," Davey said. "I wouldn't treat a stray dog like that. You ought to be ashamed of yourselves."

The Groot family glared at Davey. None of them spoke up in their defense.

"I think you all ought to cool off for a while. Get your tempers under control." He waited for an objection, but surprisingly, none came. "Here's what I intend to do, folks. Like it or not."

"You have no right to do anything," Hans said, once again belligerent. "I have ordered you off my property. If you do not go, I will shoot you."

Davey smiled, took five quick steps, rammed his rifle barrel in Hans's gut, and jerked the Dutchman's rifle from his hands. "I ought to wrap this around your neck."

Hans looked bewildered. It had all happened so fast that it almost seemed as if the disarming had not yet registered in his brain. But Kris also acted quickly and swung the hoe at Davey's head. The handle struck him behind the ear, at the back of his skull, and he staggered to the side. Seeing an opportunity, Maddy struck him with her rake and Davey went down on one knee.

"Kill him," Hans said, and leaped on top of Davey, trying to drive him into the ground. Davey brought the barrel of his own rifle up and smashed his attacker at the base of his chin. Hans tipped backward against Maddy as Kris came wading in, hammering at Davey with his fists.

Davey warded off the first blow with Hans's rifle. The second swing caught him in the nose and lights flashed in his brain like a swarm of fireflies. Kris grabbed his father's rifle by the barrel and jerked it free of Davey's grip.

As he was doing this Sheila let out a scream and started

toward the fray, crossing the porch in three steps. Davey jerked his rifle off the ground and swung the barrel toward Kris like a spear. It caught the boy in the stomach, knocking the wind from his lungs.

As Kris doubled over in pain Maddy pushed her husband back on his feet and lifted the rake up to smash Davey with the prongs.

"Shoot him, Kris," she screamed as her rake clanged on Davey's rifle barrel, knocking it downward. The shock of the blow streaked through to Davey's palms, making them sting.

Still charging, Sheila grabbed Kris by the hair and pulled him away from the fight. He turned and backhanded her across the face, sending her reeling.

Davey sidled away from his attackers and regained his footing. He swung his rifle by the barrel, landing the butt of it square on Hans's jaw. The Dutchman fell as if poleaxed, dropping to his knees, stunned. Maddy chose that moment to swing her rake at Davey and the prongs slammed into his left shoulder, but did not break the skin.

Davey turned his rifle around and lifted it high in the air. He came down with the butt end on Kris's head and the young man staggered away, took two steps, and slumped to the ground in a daze, landing in a squat that anchored him to the spot like some strange white-faced statue.

Maddy turned on Sheila and lifted the rake, ready to strike a death-dealing blow, but Davey was able to step in behind her and raise his rifle, which he brought down in front of her neck and pulled back hard. Choking for breath, Maddy dropped the rake and fell flat on her back.

Hans struggled to rise up, and Davey rammed his rifle muzzle into the Dutchman's mouth. Blood streamed from his lips and he stared up at the trapper in confusion and fear, his eyes wide.

"One more move from you, Groot," Davey warned,

"and I'll blow your brains out the back of your head. Do you understand?"

Hans nodded slightly, dumbstruck.

"Maddy, you and Kris turn over and lie flat on your bellies or you can scrape up Hans's brains with a spoon."

Mother and son quickly did as they were told.

Sheila, panting from her efforts in the fight, stood numbly to one side, her chest heaving with every painful breath.

"Sheila, you go get your things like I told you," Davey told her, also panting for breath. "Hans, you just hold real still. This rifle's cocked and my finger's tight on the trigger."

The Dutchman did not move. Maddy and Kris lay face-down, unmoving as well.

Sheila still stood there, transfixed by the results of the violent spectacle she had just witnessed. She had never seen the Groots in a subservient position before, and she was too shocked by the sight to speak. Davey looked at her questioningly.

"Sheila?" he said quietly.

"I—I don't know what to do," she whispered.

"I'll tell you what we're going to do. Groot, you need some time to think about how you've been treating this girl. She's not a slave, she's a human being. I think you all need to cool off and get a grip on your tempers. I have to go into the mountains for a few days. Sheila is coming with me."

Maddy lifted her head from the ground. "You can't do that."

"I can and I am. When I return, you'd better promise to treat her better, or I'll take her away for good."

"Mister, that is kidnapping, and you will go to the jail, I think, for stealing something that belongs to me." Hans was regaining his former bravado.

"There's no law out here," Davey said. "Besides, I'm not stealing Sheila. I'm just borrowing her for a few days."

He turned to glance at the girl. "That okay with you, Sheila?"

"You better not go," Maddy warned.

"Or what?" Sheila asked. "You will punish me? You will beat me again?"

"That is right," Maddy said.

"See?" Davey grimaced with contempt. "You don't learn very quick, do you? If you ever beat Sheila again, you'll have to answer to me. In other words, Groot, I'm making Sheila my business."

He gestured to Sheila, and she paused for a moment, then walked around to the side of the house where the Groots had built a small shelter for her. Davey's face wrinkled in disgust.

"You people build yourself a fort, then put Sheila outside like a dog in a doghouse. Completely unprotected."

"We watch over her," Hans said.

"You're an animal, Groot."

Sheila returned in a few minutes with a single bundle.

"That's all you have?" Davey asked.

She nodded. "This is all that I can really call my own."

"Get up on my horse," Davey told her.

"You will be sorry to do this," Hans said in his awkward English. "For this you will pay."

"As a matter of fact, I intend to pay you right now, Groot," the young trapper said. "A fair price for the loan of your bondservant."

"You—you have no right—" Maddy started to say, but her husband cut her off.

"Shut up," he said. "How much do you pay, Longworth?"

"What is her worth?"

"Why, at least a dollar a day."

"That much?" Davey asked sarcastically.

"It is fair," Hans said.

Davey laughed harshly. Hans didn't even wince. He stared at the trapper with unblinking eyes, and Davey felt his stomach turn with disgust. Sheila climbed onto the saddle of Davey's horse and scooted over the cantle, clutching her bundle of clothes and personal articles.

"I'll pay you when we get back," Davey told Groot. "We're leaving now, but I want you to all have a good talk about your obligations to Sheila, and how a human being should be treated."

"We do not mistreat her," Maddy said. "She is going to be our daughter soon."

"We'll talk about that, too, when I get back," Davey promised. "Now stay put until we're gone. If any of you moves before I'm across the Platte, I'll put a lead ball in your brisket. You hear me, Hans?"

"You give us the money when you get back," Hans said. "Then we talk."

Davey turned and climbed into the saddle. The mules balked at first, but he jerked on the lead rope and they promptly fell into step behind the horse. As they began to move off, Sheila turned and looked back.

"They're not moving," she said.

Davey laughed.

"You enjoy this, don't you?" Sheila asked.

"Not much. I just can't abide the way the Groots treat you."

"That is their right," she said.

"Well, we can talk about that. You're not afraid to be alone with me, are you?"

"Maybe. Should I be?"

Davey laughed again. They approached a ford and Sheila gripped him tightly around his waist.

"I promise not to beat you," Davey said. "If you behave."

"What's that supposed to mean?"

"It means that I'll treat you kindly. Now hold on, we've a river to cross."

The South Platte was still running hard and muddy from the spring snowmelt and the fording was precarious as the current tried to pull the horse and mules downstream. Sheila clung ever more tightly to Davey's waist and moments later they struck shore and emerged without getting wet. The horse shook off the water from its belly and legs and the mules tried to find a place to wallow and dry off.

"We made it." Sheila sighed.

"Did you think we wouldn't?" Davey laughed.

Sheila gave him a squeeze. He patted the back of her right hand. "I wasn't worried," she said.

"Good. I like a woman with grit."

"Grit?"

"Something like courage," Davey explained.

But say what he would, Sheila knew she had never been so frightened in her life. She was afraid of being alone with a man she did not know, and she was fearful of the consequences of her behavior when and if she was returned to the Groot family. At the same time, though, she was relieved to be away from them for a while. Who knows, she thought, maybe they would change. She took a breath and made a vow to herself.

If the Groot family did not treat her better, she would run away. But she wouldn't tell this to Davey. She was thinking of Eagle Heart, wondering if he would help her when the time came to escape from the Groot homestead.

Chapter
Twenty-Four

Peaches heard someone calling his name in a loud whisper and the sound startled him. He had thought he was all alone in the fringe of timber a few hundred yards below the rimrock.

He did not answer right away, because he thought the voice was no more than a trick of the ears. He had often heard odd sounds in the mountains, whispered words born of wind or rain, echoes of conversations that arose out of tree stumps and along creeks, conversations that had never been carried on by humans. So he stopped, listened, checked the powder in his pan, and fingered the hammer of his rifle, ready to bring it to full cock.

Again someone called to him and this time the whisper was louder and unmistakably human.

"Who's there?" Peaches called out, and then rode his horse behind a large pine for protection.

"It's me, Tall Tom, and John Cleel."

"Show yourselves," Peaches brayed.

Several men rode out of the junipers and firs, headed by Tall Tom and John Cleel. Peaches felt a wave of shock roll through him like an earthquake tremor.

"How did . . ."

"John, he got us back together," Tall Tom said. "Slick as anything."

"There are still more of our men scattered," Cleel added. "If we find 'em, we've got enough men to mount another attack. Now that we know where them damned Utes are."

"Hell," Peaches coughed, "that's just plain suicide."

"The Utes are scattered, too," John said. "We can pick 'em off one by one."

"Why, that's just plumb crazy, John." Peaches grimaced at this foolhardiness. "We'd better get back to Cherry Creek while we still got hair to comb."

"Either way, we can't leave those other men at the mercy of the savages."

"Where do you figger to look?" Peaches asked.

Tall Tom spoke up. "We figger there's a half dozen or so within a quarter mile. We just got to ride easy through the timber and keep our eyes peelt."

Peaches thought for a moment. "I guess it's the least we can do. Where do we look for the stragglers?"

"Just follow me and Tall Tom," Cleel said.

Tall Tom doubled back in a circle the way Peaches had come, and the odd procession meandered in and out of dense clumps of trees and brush, pausing often to listen for sounds.

An hour later they came upon a grisly sight. Three of their number had been scalped and decapitated, and their genitals cut away, their bodies mutilated beyond recognition. Some of the men following Cleel got sick and threw up what had once been breakfast. The stench from the torn entrails and the vomit drove the men off, considerably dampening their earlier enthusiasm.

Cleel turned his horse away from the carnage, but Peaches lingered, studying the tracks around the place where the men had died.

"You coming?" Tall Tom called, when he saw that Peaches was the only man staying behind.

"In a minute."

"Hurry up." Tall Tom rode a few steps, then turned his horse again. "What you got?" he asked.

"Just lookin' around," Peaches said.

Tall Tom rode back to where Peaches was studying the ground, the dead men.

"Those men were dragged here." Peaches pointed to the drag swaths in the ground. "Look at their clothes, the sides of their faces."

"Still alive?"

"Yep," Peaches replied. He rode around in a circle, gradually widening it to study all the tracks in the area. "And on their own horses."

Tall Tom leaned over from his saddle and then sat up straight. "'Pears to be," he said.

"And where is Cleel going?"

"Why, he's afollerin' them shod-horse tracks."

"I don't like it," Peaches muttered.

"How come?"

"Seems to me them Utes laid down that trail in particular. They want us to foller 'em."

"Hmmm." Tall Tom studied the tracks more carefully now. He and Peaches became absorbed in their activity, drifting farther apart, then coming back together. Finally they stopped their horses alongside one another.

"Well, what ya think, Peaches?"

"Look at them dead men there, Tall Tom."

"Hideous. I can't look at 'em."

"Well, their mouths are stuffed full of dirt."

"Maybe from bein' dragged from up yonder," Tall Tom suggested, a tentative edge to his voice.

"Nope." Peaches shook his head. "Deliberately poured in them dead mouths."

"What for?"

"Old Injun warning I heard about. Means the land belongs to the Utes and not the white man. Meaning the oniliest way we get any of the land is to eat it and die."

"Jesus," Tall Tom breathed, shivering involuntarily. He looked around the woods, as if expecting Utes to erupt from the shadows at any moment. "Let's get the hell out of here."

"Yep," Peaches agreed, "but wait a minute. Let's think about this."

"What do you mean?"

"What happened to the horses these men had?" Peaches asked.

"I reckon the Utes done stole 'em."

"Then why go down the mountain when their camp's up yonder?"

"Hell, Peaches, I don't know and I don't really give a tinker's goddamn."

"Could be they want us to foller them horses. Like John is adoin'."

"And jump us? Hell, they coulda done that already."

"True. But they didn't. So why lead us down the mountain?"

"Beats the shit out of me, Peaches."

"I think Cleel knows what's acomin'."

"What?"

"I think Cleel read this sign good as you and me. I was studyin' him when he was here. He acted like he warn't payin' no attention but he was readin' sign. You seen any pony tracks here?"

"No."

"So they dragged them boys here of a purpose and brung their horses and now are agettin' us to foller 'em."

"Well, why in hell wouldn't Cleel have gone on and tolt us that?"

"Because I think John is going to lead us right smack into the Utes and then light a shuck for Cherry Creek."

"Yeah?"

"Yeah, Tall Tom. All by his lonesome."

"Christ, Peaches, you sure as hell got an active imagination."

"Well, let's just catch up to John and the others and see. You be ready to foller me if we get jumped by a passel of Utes."

"Hell, Peaches."

"You be ready, Tall Tom, or you'll be dead like these fellers."

The two men rode away from the place of death, each deep in his own thoughts.

Peaches was pretty sure that the Utes had wanted their enemies to see their brothers like that. More and more as they rode he had the feeling that they were riding into a trap. However, none but Cleel was leading them, so how could that be? Maybe the Utes were smarter than anyone thought.

One thing was sure. Peaches did not trust John Cleel.

Finally, he and Tall Tom caught up with the group of men. All along the way Peaches found confirmation for his belief that they were following the tracks of the dead men's shod horses.

"What you boys been up to back there?" Cleel demanded.

"Just lookin' around," Tall Tom said.

"Havin' a smoke," Peaches added. Actually he wanted to fill his pipe pretty badly right then.

"Yeah? See anything?" Cleel asked, deliberately casual.

"Just a lot of tracks," Tall Tom replied.

"Well, that's what we're adoin'," Cleel said. "Tryin' to find the rest of our bunch. These horses might lead us to the others."

"That what you think?" Peaches asked innocently.

"Could be," Cleel answered, and that was the moment when Peaches knew he was lying.

He said nothing, but noticed that the tracks of the shod horses showed them carrying weights and there were no moccasin tracks on the trail. The Utes were riding those horses and they weren't going to lead their enemies to any remaining survivors.

On a hunch, Peaches ranged wide of the trail on both sides, scanning all the while, and what he saw confirmed his suspicions.

On one side of the trail, there were the tracks of unshod ponies.

The Utes were somewhere close by, waiting for them. Waiting to finish them off.

And he'd bet any amount of money that John Cleel knew what was bound to happen.

Chapter
Twenty-Five

D avey rode to the confluence of the two rivers, that junction where the Cache de Poudre spills into the South Platte, then he turned the horse upstream, following the Poudre until it made a bend. There, he stopped in a wide meadow where the grass was deep and lush.

"We'll graze the horse and mules here," he said.

Sheila sighed. Her grip on his waist had not been so tight once they were on dry land, but the warmth of her touch lingered as she pulled her hands away. Davey helped her step down from the saddle, holding her arm as she put her left foot in the stirrup and swung her right leg around, landing lightly.

"You've ridden a horse before," Davey observed.

"Yes. I love horses."

He stepped down from the saddle and stretched his arms, took a deep breath as he gazed at the mountains towering above them.

"How far do we have to go?" Sheila asked, flexing her fingers to take away the stiffness.

"We've got a five- or six-hour ride," Davey said. "Not far."

"Seems like a long way."

"You move slow in the mountains."

"You like it up here, don't you?"

"It's hard for me to come down from the mountains in the spring. There's a sadness in leaving what has been home."

Davey put loose hobbles on the horse and mules, loosened the bit on the horse's bridle. He didn't want to give up all control in case a bear or some other creature startled them. The mules remained on the lead rope tied to the saddle horn.

"Davey."

The young trapper turned around. Sheila stood there in the meadow, her hair on fire, her blue eyes bright as periwinkles. She was trembling.

"What is it?" he asked.

"I—I'm scared."

"Scared of what? Me?"

"I don't know. You, Hans, Maddy, Kris. Everything."

"I'm not going to hurt you. And you don't have to worry about the Groots for a while."

"But what about when I get back?"

"We'll handle that when we come to it."

"We're all alone out here," she said.

Davey looked puzzled. "So?"

"You might take advantage of me."

He laughed. "I could at that. But I won't. This is strictly a mission of mercy."

"Don't you have a girl?"

"Nope."

"Did you ever?"

Davey's face darkened. "I was sweet on a girl once."

"What happened?"

"Nothing. My pa, he thought work was more important than sparking a gal, I reckon."

"Did you go to school?"

"Nope. My ma, she taught me at home."

Hearing his words, Sheila seemed to relax. She moved closer to Davey, who had stooped to rip up a blade of grass. He stuck the green shoot into his mouth and started chewing on it.

"What did she teach you?"

"To read and write. Some arithmetic. The Bible."

"My mother taught me, too."

"That's good."

"I read storybooks and such. She didn't read the Bible."

"Too bad. Some good stories in there."

"Maybe someday I'll read it."

Davey said nothing. He was listening to birdcalls and trying to distinguish other sounds. He heard the snort of an elk, and on a higher ridge, he saw a mule deer standing almost in the open.

Sheila studied him for a long time, picked a shoot of grass for herself, and chewed on it. It tasted sweet at first, then turned sour. But there was something very satisfying about the juices in her mouth.

"You really love it up here, don't you?" she asked.

"I can't get enough of it."

"I feel so lost. So—so far away from everything. It's . . . a little scary."

"The more I see of what men call civilization, the more I like it out here," Davey said.

"But there's no one else around, no one to talk to if you're all alone."

Davey nodded in agreement. "It can get to you, the lonesomeness, but once you go into the woods, the mountains, then it comes into you."

"You talk strange, Davey."

He laughed. "I suppose. I don't talk to people much."

"No, I mean, you seem to know what you want and you're educated and everything."

"My education doesn't mean much up here. But"—he pointed a finger at his head—"it means a lot up here."

Sheila laughed. "Yes, you are a strange man."

"I'll take that as a compliment," he said, smiling.

When the horse and mules had grazed for the better part of an hour, Davey helped Sheila back onto the saddle. She sat behind the cantle as he climbed up front of her.

"Not very comfortable for you," he observed.

"I'm comfortable."

They rode out of the meadow and along the rugged shore of the Poudre, the horse picking its way through the rocks and boulders. They rode through sun-shot aspen and breathed the piney air, heavy with the scent of balsam. In the shade it was chilly, and Sheila shivered and held more tightly to Davey.

"It's so quiet," she said. "So odd not to see anyone else. We're all by ourselves."

"Oh, we have company."

She froze at these words.

"We do? Who?"

"Ever since we crossed the South Platte, we've had someone following us."

Sheila turned her head from right to left, looking for movement. "I don't see anyone."

"And you won't, until they want you to see them."

"There's more than one?"

"Yes," Davey said.

"You're not worried."

"No."

Puzzled, she pondered what Davey had told her. There must be Indians following them. But he did not seem worried, so he must know them. Could it be Eagle Heart lurking out there? Her pulse leaped at the thought.

Davey followed a dim trail along the Poudre, sometimes

going into thick timber only to emerge in bright sunlight and a dazzling greensward. Sheila marveled at the beauty of the mountains, looked long at the high snowcapped peaks, and watched the play of sun and shadow in the bristling aspens.

"What are those pretty blue flowers called?" she asked.

"I don't know."

"I've never seen any like them."

"Me neither," Davey said.

The climb became steeper and the trail twisted in and out of the timber. Two hours of riding had left Sheila feeling lost and bewildered. She wondered how Davey could find his way in such a maze of trees and rocks and mountains that seemed different at every turn.

She became even more disoriented as they entered a maze of canyons, cutbacks, stands of timber, and small glades. It occurred to her that Davey might be trying to throw whoever was following them off his trail. But he did not seem concerned and did not look back until they reached a place where the river was broken by huge boulders and formed two streams, both of them roaring down the canyon with a fury she had never seen before.

"We'll make camp here," Davey announced. "Spend the night."

"Is your cache near here?"

"Yes, very close."

"Why don't you just find your furs and go back?"

"It gets dark early in the mountains and I have to hunt. I didn't resupply at Cherry Creek, so I'm low on provisions."

"I brought some coffee," she said. "Some fatback and flour. It was all I could get in such a hurry."

"Coffee? You're an angel."

Sheila smiled. "I know you like coffee. So do I. Maddy will be furious."

"Light down," Davey said. "We won't worry about Maddy now."

"No," she said, and smiled again as she climbed down out of the saddle. She had sore spots on her calves and her buttocks were tender after the long ride. She looked at the sky and saw that they were closed in by mountains. It was cold in the shade and she shivered as the sun disappeared behind a large fluffy white cloud.

"I'll show you a place to make camp," Davey said, "and then I've got to do some hunting."

"You'll leave me alone?"

"You'll be all right. I lost my shadow for a time."

"Do you know who is following us?"

"I have a pretty good idea."

"Who?"

"I'd rather not say right now, Sheila. I could be wrong."

"Why did you lose him, then?"

"I wanted him to know I knew he was there."

"Why?"

"If it's an enemy, then he will be careful and I'll have time to see him. If a friend, he'll know I'm not taking anything for granted. A little respect, maybe."

"I see," she said.

Sheila looked around and saw that Davey had chosen a good spot to camp. The river streamed past them more than a hundred yards away, so all she heard was the rush of the water. The walls of the mountain jutted out so that the river had to make a sharp bend and no one could approach from that direction. The trees hid their camp and below them was a long open stretch of rocky terrain that stretched to the next bend of the river. There was only one approach from below, another through steep ground thick with timber.

"Stay in the trees," Davey told her as they finished up making camp. He had set out two places to sleep, and Sheila chose one for herself. She had brought a blanket and some extra socks and a change of dress. Davey had given her another blanket, marked a spot where she was to set her fire, and laid out some of his larder. "Stay as quiet as you can, and if you need help, just yell out. I won't be far away."

"Don't be too long," she said, a tremor edging her voice.

Davey disappeared into the timber and Sheila was alone. For a time she watched the horse and the mules graze, saw them fight for a clump of grass, the gelding nudging the mules away, laying back his ears and slashing at them with his bowed neck. Then she began to gather firewood, keeping close to the campsite. She made a little ring of stones and, finding a small pick in Davey's saddlebag, dug out a hole and began laying in kindling.

After she laid out possible items for supper and arranged the few cooking utensils she found in Davey's saddlebags, she walked to the Poudre. Ice and snow still floated downstream from the high reaches of the Rocky Mountains and she tossed a couple of pebbles into the rushing waters. Out of the corner of her eye she saw something gleaming some yards upstream where the river made a bend around the outcrop of mountain.

The closer she got to the shining object, the more puzzling it became. As she drew still closer yet she realized that it was not a single object, but several, all neatly arranged, by some human hand it seemed, atop a large boulder.

As she came to within fifteen yards the horror of what she was looking at struck her and she screamed. At the same time, off in the distance, she heard the crack of a rifle, and although there was no connection between what she heard and what she saw, the blood drained from her brain in a sudden rush and she sank to her knees, light-headed.

She looked upward, as if transfixed by what she had seen, and the row of human skulls all seemed to be looking down at her and grinning.

Sheila fainted before she could let out another scream.

Chapter
Twenty-Six

John Cleel seemed nervous. He rallied the men with words of encouragement, then left them to forge ahead while he told them he was going to check their flanks. Peaches noticed this behavior from well in the rear of the straggling survivors of the Ute attack, but said nothing for a time.

"Tall Tom, don't you think that John Cleel is acting mighty peculiar?" Peaches finally asked, when Cleel had disappeared again.

"I don't know. I reckon he's bein' careful."

"Careful, my royal ass. He's gettin' ready to run like a rabbit."

"To where? Hell, we're all lost as hell. Onliest thing I know is we're goin' downhill to get out of these damned mountains."

"That's what's bothering me," Peaches said. "He told us he's lookin' to pick up the others who got out of the fight, but they wouldn't be down this far. They'd be back up the mountain, probably holed up."

"Could be," Tall Tom admitted.

"Let's watch Cleel real close."

The two trappers kept their distance, riding well to the rear of the others, even though Cleel urged them to stay close.

"We'll be right near," Peaches told him.

The ride was slow and twisting through downed timber, lightning-struck deadfalls, through brush, and at times on hardpan in the open. But most of the time neither Peaches nor Tall Tom could see more than ten yards ahead and they were careful to look in all directions and keep their silhouettes low.

Cleel and his men broke through the timber late in the afternoon and emerged onto a wide grassy plateau. The first man to ride out took an arrow square in his chest. He kept riding for a few yards, soundless as his blood welled up in his throat, then tumbled from his horse. The other men scattered, brandishing their rifles and yelling.

Cleel backed up into the timber and turned his horse. Peaches and Tall Tom stopped their horses and stared at him with accusing eyes.

"Where you goin', John?" Peaches asked.

"I'm gettin' the hell out of here."

"I thought you come up here to fight."

"There's no chance."

"You knew that goin' in," Peaches told him, grim-faced.

"Get out of my way," Cleel ordered, drawing his pistol from his belt.

Tall Tom was right in Cleel's path and he held his horse reined in tight as he reached for his rifle. Cleel fired at him at point-blank range. Peaches brought his own rifle up to his shoulder, but Cleel knocked it aside and rode past at a fast lope. Before Peaches could recover, the man was gone, and Tall Tom was reeling in the saddle, trying to keep from falling as blood spurted from a ragged hole in his chest.

"God, Peaches," Tall Tom groaned, "he done shot me."

Peaches rode up next to Tall Tom and reached out for him with his free hand. He steadied his friend in the saddle, propping him up as he swayed back and forth. He heard the rattle of blood in Tom's throat and saw the blood gushing from his chest and back. He knew, without touching, that he could put his hand inside the exit hole in Tall Tom's back.

"Swing over and I'll help you down."

"I'm done for, Peach." Tall Tom attempted to say something else, but the words were lost in a gurgle of blood.

Tall Tom leaned toward Peaches and closed his eyes. The trapper-turned-prospector eased him out of the saddle, but knew there was nothing he could do for his friend. Tall Tom was dead before his feet hit the ground.

Peaches hung on for a moment, then let Tall Tom's body slide down his leg. The corpse crumpled in a lifeless heap and Peaches looked at him one last time. "So long, old friend," he said.

Then he turned his horse and started following Cleel's trail. He was surprised after a time to see that John was headed back toward the plateau where the Utes had attacked.

Cleel had made no effort to hide his tracks. He was a man in a hurry and this puzzled Peaches. He asked himself: What do I know about John Cleel? What kind of a man is he? He had heard, of course, that Cleel had been a dockwalloper in New Orleans, that he had been in some fights, had killed at least one man, perhaps more. He seemed to want to lead men, and he had convinced not only Peaches, but others, that he could take care of the Ute problem.

Now Peaches was seriously questioning Cleel's motives in launching this disastrous expedition. The man had told everyone that he was a geologist and knew from reading the rocks and soil that there was gold in the South Platte and in the mountains. The other prospectors believed him. Peaches had met him the previous spring and had been suspicious of him then. But if there was indeed gold in the region, he didn't want to be left out. While no prospector had found any significant amount of color, Peaches had found enough placer gold to keep him looking.

There was something about gold that gave a man the fever. Once he saw the glitter of gold flakes in a mining pan, snugged up bright against the black of the dolomite, he became gripped with that strange gold fever. Peaches had seen gold once, and it held a strange and powerful fascination for him.

As the former trapper rode higher and higher he became convinced that Cleel was returning to the plateau where some of their number had been killed. An hour later he came to the place, riding up on a long sidehill slantwise so that he wouldn't have to lead his horse up the steep rimrock.

A stiff breeze was blowing and it whipped the clothing of the dead men, who lay where they had fallen on the edge of the plateau. Their horses were gone.

He recognized Cal Hoddings and Jasper Reed, Carlos Sanchez and Dan Smith, men he had known only a short time, three, four days, a week, and some men whose names he did not know but recognized from sight, and others he did not know at all. Men gone from the face of the earth, left to rot and go back to the soil or fill the bellies of coyotes, wolves, vultures, worms, and ravenous insects.

Peaches rode to the first man and looked at him. Like the others, he had been scalped, but he saw no signs of mutilation. Curiously, though, the man's pockets were turned inside out.

"That's mighty strange," Peaches said to no one.

Boots, belts, hats, all were missing from the dead men, as well as knives, pistols, rifles.

The Utes could have taken these things, of course, but Peaches wondered if they would have had time if they were still chasing the survivors, as he believed them to be.

Peaches' stomach roiled. He turned his horse away from the carnage and sacking and rode back the way he had come. He rode down through the desolate quietness of an abandoned mountain as if leaving a graveyard that had been uprooted and decimated. He felt faint and giddy, not only from the altitude, but from the horrible realization that Cleel was a man rotting inside, a man so consumed by a coldness of feeling for his fellowman that he seemed no longer human.

A short time later Peaches was not surprised to come across the tracks of Cleel's horse once again, this time heading back down the mountain. The tracks were so fresh the steam arose from them like smoking brimstone. The horse droppings were also fresh, green and smoking, ravaged by deerflies and gnats.

With a sickening dread at what he might find at the site of the last ambush, the former trapper rode on, careful to stop and listen for sounds made by men or horses. But the silence only deepened, and as it did so, it increased the dread inside him, and when he returned to the place where Cleel had shot Tall Tom, the dread was replaced by anger.

Tom had not been scalped, but he had been robbed. Peaches knew that Tall Tom's pockets had been filled with money from the sale of his winter furs and now they were turned out, like the pockets of the others left on the plateau, and his belt, shoes, and pistol, his rifle, all were gone, as well as his horse.

Peaches found signs that Cleel had stripped Tom's horse of its saddle, probably packed all the stolen goods on the dead trapper's horse, then put the saddle on top. So now Cleel had a packhorse and the plunder from dead men.

Where would he go with his booty? Peaches knew that he would probably not return to Cherry Creek, and if he did, it would only be to spread lies about the fight with the Utes.

A few moments later he arrived at the glade where the vanguard of prospectors had been ambushed. He waited cautiously at the edge, holding his horse tight against a backdrop of fir trees and pines. He waited and listened.

Again he saw the flap of loose clothing stirred by the vagrant mountain breezes, and when he looked closely, he noticed that the dead men had been scalped. Not a man of those who had made it through the earlier attack had survived, at least as near as he could tell. They all lay within a few yards of each other.

Cleel had already done his dirty work there, too. The scalped corpses had been stripped of useful clothing, money, boots, and shoes.

"A ghoul," Peaches muttered. "That's what Cleel is, a goddamned ghoul." It was a word he had never used before, but he knew what it meant. He had heard of grave robbers before. It was one of mankind's oldest and least admirable practices.

Peaches rode on, and by the time he cleared the meadow he knew that Cleel had picked up two more horses to carry his plunder. He could also tell that the Utes had gone back up the mountain, apparently satisfied with their victories, and none followed Cleel or waited ahead in ambush.

"I'll bet you wish they had got me, too, mister," Peaches said. "Well, they didn't, and by God, I'm going to get you, you son of a bitch."

Late in the day he learned something else about John Cleel. The man was not returning to Cherry Creek, but was giving it a wide berth. His tracks had veered to the northeast. His path would intersect the South Platte and Peaches wondered which way he would head when he reached the river, another day's long slow ride.

"Don't make no damned difference where you go, Cleel. I'm going to find you and make sure you die real slow, slow enough to beg for mercy."

It was a thought that kept the trapper-turned-prospector going long into the afternoon, even into the night. And when he made camp, he thought he saw a flickering campfire in the darkness far below and he wondered if Cleel was eating dead men's food and counting their stolen money.

Chapter
Twenty-Seven

Davey had been watching the yearling mule deer for the better part of ten minutes. The animal was grazing in a copse of trees, shielded from a clear shot. Its big gray ears twitched and flicked off flies, its rubbery nostrils wrinkled and bent to catch any vagrant scent.

Davey eased back the set trigger while he held the hammer a notch back, then leaned the barrel against the pine where he stood, placing it at eye level for a quick shot when the deer moved out into the open.

The trapper glanced around without moving his head to see if any other deer were grazing nearby. He could see only a few yards, but he thought the yearling was probably alone. He waited, and finally the yearling stepped out into the open, a shaft of sunlight catching the creature in its beam.

Davey held his breath and pulled the hammer back to full cock. He squeezed the trigger and the rifle bucked against his shoulder. A billowing spool of white smoke belched from the muzzle and for a moment the deer was obscured from his sight. But he heard the ball hit home with a dull thud and underneath the smoke he saw the deer twist and fall on its hind legs. It struggled to rise, then collapsed onto its forelegs.

That was when Davey heard the scream. Sheila's scream. It tore through him like red flags unfurling in a blistering wind. He turned. reloading his rifle on the run, his heart pounding in his chest like ragged thunder.

Then the scream stopped and it was quiet as Davey ran headlong through the timber, ramming the ball home then flipping the rifle, pouring fine powder into the pan like splashing water. But he knew enough of the powder would cling to the brass to spark when the flint struck the frizzen. He capped the small powder horn with thumb and forefinger and righted the rifle, ready to fire from the hip if necessary.

He tried to pinpoint the source of the scream and angled toward the Poudre, just above their camp. He figured that Sheila's voice had bounced off the sheer bluffs above the river bend and that she was somewhere near the water.

Davey broke into the open and saw Sheila's crumpled body lying on the rocks. He heaved a sigh of relief when he saw the huge boulder with its hideous array of human skulls. He knew then what had happened and had to stifle a laugh. It would not be funny to Sheila, he knew. It must have given her quite a start to see those skulls gleaming white in the shimmering sunlight.

Davey knelt next to the girl and laid his rifle alongside after peering around to see if they were alone. He picked her up gently in his arms and lightly tapped her cheeks, which were drained of color.

"Hey, wake up," he said.

Sheila moaned and her eyelids fluttered.

"It's okay," Davey said, propping her up.

"Huh?" She opened her eyes and stared at him with a look of disbelief. "Wha—what happened? Where am I?"

"You fainted, I reckon."

Sheila's eyes widened with understanding. She pointed to the skulls. "That's what scared me," she said.

"I know. Pretty bad thing to see if you're not expecting it."

"Who are they? Indians?"

Davey shook his head. "Frenchmen, I hear. Long time ago. They cached their furs here and I guess they made the Utes mad. The Utes killed 'em and put their skulls up there to warn off other trappers."

"But you came here," she said.

"It's a good place to cache furs. I reckon the Utes figured if I wasn't afraid, then I must have some powerful medicine."

"Medicine?" She looked at him questioningly.

"Power, good spirit. Like that medicine pouch Eagle Heart gave you. Brings good luck."

Sheila suddenly realized that Davey's arms were around her and became embarrassed. She tried to get up and toppled back into the trapper's lap.

"Here, I'll help you," he said. "Do you want a drink of water?"

"Yes, yes, that would be fine," she replied quickly, using Davey's arm to pull herself to her feet.

"Let's walk back to camp and I'll get the canteen."

They walked away from the river together, but not close. Sheila seemed to want to keep her distance from him.

Later Davey retrieved the deer he had shot, skinned it in camp, removed its innards, and cut steaks and ribs out. He started the fire as the sun stood gleaming just above the snowcaps and Sheila put on a coat and stood near the flames to keep warm.

Davey made bannock in the skillet with flour and drippings from the roasting meat.

"Mmm, it smells good," Sheila said.

"It'll taste mighty good, too. I'll put up a lean-to where we can sleep tonight."

"We—we're sleeping together?"

"Sort of. Easier to keep warm that way. It'll be a frosty night. The sky's clear and we're pretty high up."

"I don't know if that's proper," she said.

"Proper or not, you'll welcome the heat."

"You won't do anything, will you?"

"Nothing you don't want me to," Davey said, grinning.

"I don't want you to do anything."

"Fine with me, Sheila."

They spoke little during supper. Sheila ate heartily and Davey was pleased. The deer carcass hung from a tree high above the ground, well away from wolves and bears. He had seen no bears yet, but he knew they'd be coming out of their dens soon, and when they did, they'd be starving for any kind of food.

After supper, Davey washed the skillet in the Poudre with sand and water, stoked up the fire. Then he pitched a lean-to with a canvas tarp and laid out their bedrolls. "You can use your clothes for a pillow," he told Sheila.

"I'm not sleepy," she announced.

Davey laughed. "We'll sit by the fire and watch all the stars come out. You'll be sleepy soon."

"Well, I'm kind of sleepy."

"Me, too," Davey said. "This mountain air will put you down."

"Do you want me to make coffee?" she asked.

"Morning will be fine."

"Will we be going back tomorrow?"

"Maybe the next day. I've got two caches up here, mine and a friend's who was killed by the Utes just before I came down the last time."

"Killed? What happened to him?"

Davey told her about Caleb Wakefield, how he had found him and how he had died.

"That's awful," she said when he finished.

"Dying is painful for everyone."

"Are you afraid of dying, Davey?"

He took out his pipe, filled it with tobacco, and lit it with a faggot from the fire before answering.

"Not especially."

"I am."

"What's there to be afraid of?" he asked. "Way I figure it, it's part of life. We kill critters to eat and critters kill each other. Leaves die in the fall and new ones sprout up in the spring."

"Not the same leaves," she pointed out.

Davey chuckled. "No, but life is dying as much as living. Eagle Heart explained to me how the Arapaho feel about death and I reckon he made a lot of sense."

"What did he tell you?"

"That all life is a circle. Life is never-ending."

"How can that be?" Sheila asked.

"I don't know. Maybe we live on in other forms—animal, human, plant."

"Reincarnation?"

"Big word, Sheila. But something like that, I guess."

"Well, I don't understand any of it. If you're dead, you're dead."

"Some folks hold to that, and I guess that might be. If so, then there is no reason to fear death. If you just stop being who you are, then you won't even remember who you were."

"I've never thought of it that way."

"Well, I thought of it when my folks passed on and when Caleb died. And I thought of it when I killed that deer. If we're just here for a short while, what's the purpose of life? Is it just to live and die and be done with all of it?"

"You sound like a philosopher," she said.

Davey laughed. "Well, I don't know about that, but death is pretty big in people's minds. They talk about it enough. And I guess I wonder why."

"So you think people don't just die and that's all there is," she said.

"Well, nobody knows. I think there might be something

else. The Indian thinks he goes to some happy hunting ground in the sky and then he continues on the circle and becomes a man again."

Sheila shook her head. "It's all too complicated for me. I am sleepy now."

"Boring subject, huh?"

"Not boring, just a lot of questions that can't be answered and I don't have the energy to even think of what might be after we die."

"You go ahead and go to bed," Davey said. "I'm going to wait up awhile and look around before I turn in."

"You mean stand guard?"

"I always sleep with one eye open."

"Don't scare me, Davey."

"Okay."

They spoke no more until Sheila said good night and Davey wished her a good night's sleep. He saw that she fell asleep quickly and he was glad for that. Now he was alone with the stars and the sky and the night sounds. An owl called in the distance and he heard the howl of a wolf on the prowl, dead branches crack under the footfall of deer or elk.

In the quiet, he could hear his own heart beat and the stars seemed close enough to touch. Davey stopped looking at the fire a good ten minutes before he got up and made a wide circle around their camp, stopping often to listen.

When he returned, he stayed to the shadows and watched the lean-to for a long while just to be sure no one was creeping up on it in the darkness.

Then, just before he walked to the campsite to go to bed, he heard a fluting sound, clear as crystal. It belonged to no bird he had ever heard, nor to any animal. It was just a single plaintive note that died in pools of silence, so brief, he thought he might have imagined it.

He did not hear the sound again before he fell asleep,

but he smiled as he closed his eyes. He knew that none would sneak up on them during the night. He looked over at Sheila, all bundled up in a coat, a blanket over her. A feeling of warmth suffused his body and he did not feel cold as he dropped off to sleep without a robe to warm him.

Chapter
Twenty-Eight

Hans Groot stepped back from the newly built structure, smacked his pudgy lips. "Now we have the chicken coop. Maddy, you will have fresh eggs every morning."

Kris emerged from the inside of the coop. "I'll fetch the cages with the chickens," he said.

Maddy smiled. "I am very proud of my men."

She and Kris had taken the wagon to the main settlement, where they knew they could buy chickens. There, they had visited with people they knew from Nebraska and St. Louis. They returned with two dozen chickens, including layers, breeders, and hen pullets. The birds had been cackling in close confinement for two days.

"They will be safe in this coop." Hans nodded proudly at his handiwork. "Tomorrow I put up the wire fence, eh?"

"The chickens will get plenty of air with all those fine windows." Maddy was beaming with pride as she spoke. "Fresh eggs. My, my."

Kris carried two cages to the coop, put them inside without opening them as he went to bring more cages. Suddenly he stopped, peered down the Platte over the open prairie. "Somebody is coming," he said.

Maddy and Hans looked in the direction where their son had seen someone heading their way.

"It is not the trapper," Hans said.

"No, but he looks familiar," Maddy returned. "He has three packhorses."

"A trader, maybe," Kris suggested.

"He's waving." Maddy scrunched up her skirt and wiped her hands of sweat, as if she were anxious to shake hands with the visitor. Then she waved back.

"Don't make him welcome until we know who he is," Hans warned, a sharp tone to his voice.

Maddy let her hand drop, chastised by her husband.

As the rider drew closer Hans's face turned waxen. "Do you know who that is?" he asked.

"Sure looks familiar." Kris squinted in an effort to see the approaching rider more clearly.

"I don't believe it," Maddy exclaimed. "After all this time . . ."

"Let me handle this, Maddy," Hans said.

"I don't like it at all." Maddy stared in disbelief as the rider drew still closer.

"Who is it?" Kris asked.

"You just be quiet," Hans ordered his son.

The three were silent until the rider came upon them.

"Hans, hello. Maddy. And is that young Kris? Well, he has growed some."

"John Cleel," Hans said stiffly. "What brings you way out here? We thought you went to New Orleans."

"I did go to New Orleans. Now I'm trading and I come to ask about Sheila. Where is she?"

"She is not here," Hans said.

Cleel stepped down from his horse, left the reins to trail. The other three horses stood patiently, secured to a lead rope. They bore loosely tied packs and bundles that were unrecognizable.

"Well now, maybe you got some explainin' to do," the Groots' old acquaintance began. "Remember, I'm the one what got you the girl in the first place."

"I remember," Hans said. "She will be back soon."

"Good. Her bond has run out and I aim to return her to her ma."

"She is to be—" Maddy started to say, but Hans cut her off with a stern look.

"What's that?" Cleel asked. His clothes were covered with dust and he had not shaved. The horses were obviously tired, and he looked as if he had not slept in a pair of days. His hands were stained with dried blood and he stank of something none of the Groots wanted to mention.

"Sheila and our son, Kris, are to be married soon," Maddy said. "So there."

Cleel's mouth clamped shut and his features hardened in anger and disapproval.

"She is to be our daughter," Hans added. "My son's wife."

"Well, I'll be damned." Cleel shook his head in surprise. "You people seem to have forgotten that I was the broker in this deal. I arranged for you to meet with Sheila's mother and take her daughter in servitude."

"And you were well paid, John," Hans said.

"I said I would be back to claim Sheila, too."

After a brief but uncomfortable pause Maddy spoke. "How did you find us?"

"I knew when you left St. Louis and I knew when you got here," Cleel told her. "In fact, I was right behind you."

"You followed us?" Hans was clearly taken aback by this news.

"Not exactly. I'm the one who told your friends about this territory and I helped set up the wagon train, through another man who acted as my agent."

"You're a scoundrel," Maddy said.

"Now, now, Maddy, don't say something you might be sorry for later."

"You leave Sheila alone." Kris blurted out the words before his father could silence him.

Cleel walked close to the young man and stared him down. Kris averted his gaze. "Now you listen to me, Kris. I'm coming back here for Sheila. And you're not going to marry her. Is that clear?"

Before Maddy or Hans could say a word, Cleel turned to glare at them menacingly. "I mean what I say," he added.

"You have no right," Hans said stubbornly. "Our deal was finished when we paid you for the information about Sheila's mother."

"No, our deal is finished when I get Sheila back. Her servitude to you is over, and you will owe me money for the time she worked beyond the five years."

"That is unfair," Maddy said.

"Crooked," added Hans.

Cleel's expression changed. He turned toward Hans and Maddy. "Mind your accusations," he said. "I mean to get Sheila back and you will pay me for her services since her bond ran out. What is it? A year, two?"

"We won't pay," Hans said. "Sheila is free and she will marry Kris when she returns."

"Maybe you better tell me just where she is, Hans." Cleel stood so close to Maddy and Hans that they held their breaths to keep from smelling him.

"We don't know," Maddy said quickly.

"Don't know?" Cleel's voice rose in pitch. "What do you mean you don't know?"

"She—she went away," Hans said.

"Where'd she go?"

Hans pointed up to the mountains.

"By herself?" Cleel asked.

Hans shook his head. "She went with someone. A man."

"What man?" Cleel almost shouted the question.

"A trapper. He calls himself Davey Longworth."

"Longworth?"

"That's his name," Maddy said.

"What's that bastard doing, taking Sheila up into the mountains?"

The Groots did not reply. Maddy hung her head while Kris stared into nothingness. Hans licked his dry lips.

Just at that moment a vagrant cloud passed before the sun and cast a large shadow over the homestead. The four people stood stock-still in the silence for several instants, then Cleel kicked at the dirt and scuffed up a miniature sandstorm that only emphasized the hollow stillness of the moment.

"I should have killed that bastard when I had the chance," he said finally.

"You know him?" Hans asked.

"We had a run-in," Cleel replied tightly.

Hans frowned. They had trusted Cleel once, before they had found out what a scoundrel he was. He had arranged for the purchase of Sheila as a bondservant, set up the meeting with Sheila's mother. He had taken a commission and that was supposedly the end of it. But Hans realized now that he should have known better—Cleel was like a pest you could never get rid of. Now he was back, demanding money and Sheila. He wondered if Cleel really would return her to her mother. He doubted it. Cleel was not a man to be trusted.

"You got you a nice little homestead here, Hans. I see you bought yourself some chickens. From old man Danziger?"

"Yes," Hans said.

"You have money, then?"

"We have no money. It is with the trade we got the chickens from Kurt Danziger."

"Well, you better dig up some money. I'll be back, and I'll expect you to hand over Sheila."

"Where do you go?" Hans asked.

"Why, to the settlement where all your friends are, Hans. I'll sell the goods I have here and give them fair warning not to marry Kris and Sheila." Cleel smiled as he looked at each one of the Groot family. "Fair enough?"

"You are a mean man, John Cleel," Maddy said. "Why can't you leave us alone?"

"I thought we were friends. When you wanted a bond-servant, you were eager enough to do business with me."

"We have paid you for that," Hans said. "We will not pay again."

"It would be a shame to lose all this." Cleel waved a hand to indicate the farmstead. "You got seeds in the ground, you built yourself a nice little house, and you got chickens and cows, and mules. Yes, sir, you've done well . . . with *my* help."

"We just want you to go away, John, and never come back," Hans said.

"You mind my words, Hans. I will be back and I'll want money for Sheila's services beyond the time of her bond. And she had better be here and ready to return to St. Louis."

With that, Cleel turned his back on the family and mounted his horse. Hans noticed that he looked to the south before he rode off to the east without so much as a wave of good-bye.

"I hate that man," Kris said.

"Do you hate him enough to fight him?" Hans asked.

"I hate him enough to kill him," Kris answered, and Hans smiled with grim pride.

"It might come to that," he told his son. "We just might have to kill John Cleel if he comes back here."

Maddy looked at her son and husband. Then she spoke. "It seems we have made more enemies than friends out here." Her eyes were filled with regret. "I wish we had never come."

"We are here," Hans said stubbornly. "And here we will stay."

It was then that Maddy dipped her head and covered her face with her hands. She began to weep softly and Hans did not move to comfort her.

_____ Chapter _____
Twenty-Nine

D avey put more wood on the fire. He had stirred the
coals and fed them with kindling. Then he brought
more wood to the fire ring, enough to keep the
flames going until the morning chill wore off. When the fire
blazed high, he shook Sheila awake.

"It's too cold," she said. "I don't want to get up."

"You can warm yourself by the fire, Sheila. Get a move
on. We've got to find shelter soon."

"Huh?" Sheila opened one eye and blinked up at the
trapper. "Shelter? What's wrong?"

"Take a look at that sky," he said, pointing.

Sheila sat up. It was morning and there was light, but the
sky was darkening fast. Huge lumbering black clouds moved
over the snowcapped peaks and seemed to sink down, smoth-
ering the small narrow valley where they had made camp.

"It looks like a storm's coming," she said.

"A late snowstorm," Davey agreed. "We have to move
camp right away."

"We're not going back?"

"We won't have time. If we get caught in the open,
we'd probably freeze to death. This is a big one. I've seen
them happen in June, even. The prairie will be blanketed in
snow by noon."

As if to emphasize the urgency of the situation, a few snowflakes floated down from the sky. The wind started to whip and stir the warm air, turning it chill. Sheila shivered in her coat as she bundled up the night bedding while Davey saddled his horse and set the panniers on the mules' backs.

Soon the snow was falling faster, swirling in the north wind like tiny crystal wafers in a whirlpool. Davey leaned into the brunt of the wind as he packed the bedrolls on the mules.

"Where are we going?" Sheila asked, shouting into the face of the howling wind. Davey could barely see her through the thickening wall of snow.

"There's a big cave across the river."

"How will we get across?"

"That may be tough," Davey said. "Come on, stay close to me."

"We're walking?"

"Warmer that way. Safer."

Sheila saw the logic in that. If they were sitting atop the horse, they'd be exposed to the wind. By walking, they could use the horse and mules as a buffer against it.

"How far?" she asked, after they had made their way upstream about a quarter of a mile.

"Four, five miles, maybe."

"We'll never make it." The snow was ankle-high, drifting to more than a half foot in places. She caught glimpses of the river in between gusts of wind and snow blasts. The Poudre was raging full force, rushing down the steep slope that would carry it to the North Platte.

"We've got to," Davey shouted, and bent his shoulder to the wind, pulling on his horse, feeling the slack go out of the lead rope.

Suddenly a dark shape appeared in the wind-funneled snow and Sheila grabbed Davey's arm in fear. The trapper stopped, shielded his eyes from the blowing snow.

"What is it?" she screamed.

"Don't be afraid," he said just as Eagle Heart rode up on them, his buffalo robe covered with snow, making him look like a bear on horseback.

"You come," the Arapaho leader said, leaning over so that Sheila and Davey could hear him. "Follow."

"Is that Eagle Heart?" Sheila asked. She could not be sure.

"Yes. He's been following us since we crossed the Platte. Maybe to look after you," Davey guessed.

Sheila felt her heart skip a beat and heat warm her face. She stared at the strange figure atop the pony, still not convinced that it was Eagle Heart who had spoken to them. The creature who stood before her seemed like an apparition, a ghostlike being born of the snow and icy winds.

Eagle Heart turned away from the river and rode deep into the timber where the snow was not so deep. The storm was persistent, but the wind had died. Now the snow fell in white curtains, shrouding the land in ermine, and the footfalls of the horses and mules were muffled and the tracks filled in quickly.

They began to climb, following an ancient game trail that Eagle Heart knew, but even with the wind down, it was dark and cold and Davey could feel Sheila shivering next to him. She never complained though, and they trudged on, their breath knifing into their lungs, never getting enough oxygen from the thin air to ease the pain.

Eagle Heart reached a ridge of rimrock where the trail narrowed to about two feet in width. It was slow going and the horse and mules were spooked by the danger of falling from the precipice. Finally the trail widened out and the snow did not fall so heavily since the rocks sheltered the path.

The wind shifted and threatened to blow the animals and people from the rimrock. Davey knew his horse was very frightened and patted his neck to calm him as he tried to keep Eagle Heart in sight. He saw that the Arapaho had dismounted and was leading his pony over the treacherous and slippery rock that was now covered by a layer of thin ice beneath the snow.

Eagle Heart scrambled up to a wide ledge and bore straight into a large cave, high enough for a horse to enter and a man to stand up straight. Davey and Sheila followed him inside, out of the blowing wind and snow.

The cave was large enough to accommodate all of the people and the animals, which were already shaking off the snow that had covered their coats. Davey dusted himself and Sheila off as Eagle Heart began to search the cave for kindling.

Davey joined the Indian in his search for wood. They did not speak, but began to collect small sticks that had been blown in by other winds at other times.

Sheila shivered. "Can I help?" she asked.

"Just try and stay warm," Davey told her. "We'll have a fire going in no time."

Eagle Heart piled the small sticks into a cone shape. He drew his knife and began to shave one of the sticks. Curly slivers fell to the cave floor. When he had enough, he stuck the shavings into the center of the cone. Then he signed to Davey, who nodded.

Eagle Heart stood up, then walked to the cave entrance. He did not hesitate as he marched out into the cold and snow. Sheila saw him disappear in a cloud of white flakes. She turned to Davey. "Where's he going?" she asked.

"He's going to bring in some wood. When he gets back, he'll start the fire and I'll gather some more."

"It was so nice yesterday." Sheila sighed.

"That's the mountains for you. They make their own weather. There are some high places where it's never summer."

"How awful."

Davey shrugged. "You just have to live with it," he said. "Be prepared."

"How can you prepare for such a storm?"

He laughed. "Many a man has weathered worse in the high country."

Soon Eagle Heart returned, his arms piled high with solid dry wood, pine and spruce and fir. He laid the firewood down by the cone of kindling, then retrieved a chunk of flint and a smooth round stone from his beaded pouch and began striking the flint across the widest part of the oval-shaped stone. Sparks flew into the curly shavings and ignited the dry wood.

Davey left the cave without speaking to Sheila and she stood close to Eagle Heart shivering, watching him in fascination. Soon the fire began to blaze and the Arapaho carefully nurtured the small flames, slowly piling on more kindling.

When the fire blazed high and bright, Eagle Heart started to put the larger logs on top of it in the rough shape of a tepee, one end pointed toward the center, the other at the base. At last Sheila began to feel warm. The shadows dancing on the walls of the cave were beginning to have a mesmerizing effect on her.

"The fire feels good," she said to Eagle Heart.

"Fire good."

"You speak good English, Eagle Heart."

"Yes."

Sheila smiled.

Eagle Heart smiled back at her, but she could tell it was not an expression that came easily to him. It made him all the more fascinating and endearing to her.

As the cave began to take on warmth Sheila took off her coat. She found a place to sit close to the fire, folded up her coat, and sat on it.

"I—I don't have the medicine pouch," she said.

Eagle Heart backed away from the fire and sat on his haunches. He grunted in assent.

"They—they took it from me. The Groots."

"Bad-heart Groots."

"Yes."

"They beat slave girl."

"How did you know?" She tried to hide her arms, folding them over her chest.

"Me know."

The discussion was interrupted when Davey returned with a load of wood. He set it by the other limbs and took off his coat. Then he unsaddled his horse and removed the panniers from the mules. Outside the cave the wind howled and the flames whipped with the gusts that entered and threw sparks into the air. The sparks looked like golden fireflies flung into the darkness.

"You getting warm?" Davey asked Sheila.

"Yes, very. You?"

"Right warm. You and Eagle Heart talk?"

"Some."

"He don't say much, but he thinks deep."

"We didn't talk that much."

"No, I reckon not."

"How long do you think the storm will last?"

Davey shrugged. "Hard tellin'. All day, all night. Might blow over by morning."

"I hope so. This cave smells."

"Better than being outside."

"Yes."

They both turned to see Eagle Heart stand up and walk to what appeared to be the back of the cave. Apparently it did not end there. Returning to the fire, he picked up a flaming faggot and carried it to the back of the cave as Davey and Sheila watched. The Arapaho stooped down and stuck the firebrand into a smaller hole, illuminating it for a few feet.

Something stirred in the deeper part of the cavern. They all heard a snort, then Eagle Heart stepped backward and to one side of the smaller cave.

It was then they heard another snort followed by a series of low growls.

"Bear come," Eagle Heart announced in his laconic fashion.

Davey grabbed Sheila's arm and jerked her to her feet. He pushed her to the cave wall, shielded her with his body.

Moments later a large she-grizzly lumbered from the smaller cave, snorting and grumbling, her small porcine eyes squinting at the light. She sniffed the outer cave and turned toward Davey and Sheila. She walked a few more steps, then stood on her hind legs. Davey's hand slid to the grip of the pistol stuck inside his belt.

The grizzly stood up on its hind legs and roared, its paws clawing the air. It made ugly noises in its throat and its hot stale breath permeated the air of the cave with the stench of consumed carrion. The fire popped and sparks flew up like streamers of tiny shooting stars.

Eagle Heart drew his knife without making a sound.

Then the bear dropped down and stood on all four legs.

Sheila screamed in terror as the animal charged toward her and Davey, the sound of her voice echoing in the cave in perfect counterpoint to the shrieking wind outside. A flurry of snow whirled inside and funneled to the fire, the flakes hissing as they melted in the flames.

Davey cocked his pistol, knowing it was too late for a shot to stop the bear's charge.

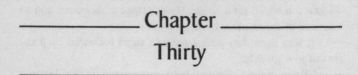

Chapter
Thirty

Fritz Stamm knew something was wrong soon after the rider from Bent's Fort arrived at the Cherry Creek digs. He rode straight for Bill Gwaltney's tent and the two stayed inside for more than an hour. The rider was a short, stocky man with a swarthy complexion, beard, buckskins, coonskin cap, two rifles, two pistols, and a small, fleet pony like the kind the Plains Indians rode.

Fritz could hear snatches of the conversation, in both French and English, but he couldn't make any sense out of it. The day before, one of the prospectors had ridden in all bloodied and babbling about the Utes and was still sleeping off the whiskey some of the other trappers had given him while trying to calm him down. This was a man named Harry Cox, a skinny, emaciated prospector who was known to be moody and on the quiet side. He looked as if he had seen a ghost, and his body bore arrow and knife wounds that marked him as one battered but lucky man.

Fritz had been waiting for Davey Longworth to return, but he hadn't shown up yet. Now an ominous pall hung over the camp, and the rider from Bent's Fort was another mystery to unravel among a bunch of men who were as curious as a barnyard full of stray cats.

Fritz whittled and smoked his pipe, all the while listening to the camp gossip, which was wild and wrong as any talk he'd ever heard. But the name John Cleel kept coming up in the conversations and he gathered Cox had mentioned it a time or two in his ravings. Nobody had any answers, though, and they all wondered what had happened to the other men who had followed Cleel in his brash assault on the Utes.

Hearing a commotion in Gwaltney's tent, Fritz looked up to see the Frenchman emerge, followed by Gwaltney. The two men shook hands. Then, to his surprise, the rider from Bent's mounted his horse and rode out of camp. Fritz watched Gwaltney, who stood there until the rider disappeared from sight. Then he returned inside his tent and Fritz could hear the banging of metal and the creak of leather.

Resisting the urge to barge in on the trader, Fritz continued to whittle and smoke his pipe. When he saw Gwaltney packing up his goods, stacking the furs he had bought in neat piles, he walked over to speak to him.

"What's up, Bill?"

"Packin' it up, Fritz."

"You goin' somewheres?"

"Back to Bent's."

"How come? Davey's got more furs he's bringin' in to sell."

"Orders from William Bent himself. I can't buy no more furs."

"What?"

Bill stopped what he was doing and looked at Fritz. "That Frenchman who rode in here told me that nobody's buying any more furs. Period."

This was strange news. "Why?"

"They're making hats out of silk now. Nobody wants beaver."

"Silk? I never heard of it."

"Me neither. I hear they got worms over there in China

that spin thread, fine thread, and the Chinks weave it into fabric. It's a god-awful thing."

"Why, sure as hell it's a god-awful thing. Worms makin' hats and such. It can't be true."

"Pierre Gaspard told me that Bent's is out of business. I'm to take the furs I bought back to the fort and get paid off. I don't know what the hell I'm going to do."

"Me neither, Bill. Christ, this is bad news. Davey will have a pure fit over this."

"Well, it can't be helped. I'm packin' it all in and then got to think what I'm goin' to do."

"Silk. Worms. Jesus."

"Yeah, I know. It don't seem fair."

Fritz helped Gwaltney pack and load his mules and then he said good-bye. Some of the other trappers wanted to know what was going on and Fritz had trouble explaining it to them. After the trader left, a mood of sadness seemed to fill the air in the camp and there was a grumbling among the men who felt sure some terrible mistake had been made. Beaver was king in the West and many of them had spent most of their grown lives standing in ice-cold streams and handling frozen traps to fetch peltries to the traders. Now they were orphans of an industry that had abandoned them.

"Looks like Davey done fetched his cache for nothing," a man named Barry Couts said. "He'll take it hard."

"Trappin's all Davey knows," Fritz said, and then, after a moment of reflecting, added, "and it's all I know, too."

"What are you going to do, Fritz?"

"I think I'll ride up the South Platte to the Poudre and tell Davey about all this."

"Like tellin' a man his wife died." Couts shook his head sadly.

"Yes, that is what it will be like, I think," Fritz agreed.

Soon the others shuffled off to be by themselves. Some

of them began to gather up their bedrolls and fold their lean-to tarps. Fritz was already saddled up and ready to ride to the South Platte when he heard Couts call out to him.

"You better hear what Cox has to say before you go," Couts said.

"He talkin' sense now?"

"He's talkin' plenty."

Fritz walked over to a circle of men gathered around Cox, who looked peaked but hale. He was drinking coffee and looking up at the men who stood over him to hear what he had to say.

"I swear I saw Cleel robbin' dead men," Cox said. "He loaded up their goods and rode off."

"How come you got away?" someone asked.

"Cleel chased me, tried to kill me. But I jumped off a little cliff and rolled down into some brush. He looked for me, but never could find me."

"It don't make no sense that Cleel would try and kill you and the others," Couts said. "Why would he do that?"

"I think he planned it all along, lookin' back on it," Cox replied. "He was hopin' we'd all get killed so's he could rob us."

"But how come he didn't get killed?" Fritz asked.

"You got me." Cox shrugged. "I been wonderin' about that myself. Maybe he made some kind of deal with the Utes. They was sure as hell waitin' for us."

Fritz thought about that. It would explain a lot of things, but it wouldn't explain how Cleel had managed to make an alliance with the Utes. He had seemed so convincing when he ranted on about punishing them, about teaching them a lesson. However, if Cleel had made a pact with the Utes, that would explain almost everything. It might even account for the smoke and mirror signals, the attack on the prospectors who were sluicing and panning the South Platte.

Come to think of it, Fritz realized, nobody knew much about Cleel, only that he had been in St. Louis and New Orleans, but so had a lot of men now in Jefferson Territory. Fritz was glad now that he had not followed Cleel after the Utes, and wondered why the others had done just that.

"You see what happened to anyone else?" he asked.

Cox shook his head. "There was so much goin' on, but like I said, it looked like Cleel led us right into the second bunch. He hung back and never did get into it. When I seen him stripping the bodies and packing dead men's possibles and such on dead men's horses, I got the hell out of there."

"You know which way Cleel went?" Couts asked.

"No," Cox said. "I stayed to the brush until I couldn't hear him thrashing around."

"One thing sure," Couts added. "He ain't comin' back here no more."

"I reckon not," someone said.

Fritz walked away, his mind crowded with thoughts. The fur trade was finished. For good, probably. And Cleel was headed somewhere to sell what he had stolen. But where? And was it any of his business anyway? Maybe. Maybe not. One thing sure. Davey had to know what was going on.

Before he could finish his thoughts, Bill Gwaltney walked up to him and asked, "Fritz, you want to ride to the fort with me?"

He thought about it for a minute or two. "I reckon I better try and find Davey Longworth, Bill."

"Suit yourself. I can pay you for the trip."

"Hell, there may not be any fort there when you get to the Arkansas."

"It'll be there."

"Someone will take you up on your offer. This place has got a smell to it now. You hear about Cleel?"

"I heard some of it. You know Cleel brought a bunch

of settlers out from St. Louis. I mean he set it all up. I wondered about it, since he didn't come with them."

"I didn't know that," Fritz said.

"He was some kind of land agent in St. Louis. Some of the settlers got lost and come by the fort. They said they didn't trust Cleel."

"But they gave him money."

"They gave him money and he sent a wagon master with them, but he abandoned them as soon as they were far enough away from St. Louis they wouldn't turn back."

"A skunk if there ever was one, that Cleel."

"Well, Fritz. I'll be seeing you, I hope."

"You be real careful, Bill. Lot of ground 'twixt here and Bent's Fort."

"Thanks, Fritz. You tell Davey I'm real sorry."

"I will. If I can find him."

With that, Gwaltney touched his fur cap and walked over to the crowd of men listening to Cox while Fritz returned to his digs and packed up his belongings. He had money in his pocket and no place to spend it. But at least he had bought food supplies and powder and ball. Davey could probably use some of it if he was still alive.

He hoped he could find his old partner. Davey was a man with a head on his shoulders and might have some ideas about what to do now that the fur trade was done with. Maybe they would prospect for gold, like the men on Cherry Creek. Davey would have some ideas; Fritz had none. He was still too shaken from all the events that had taken place in the last few hours.

Mounting his horse, Fritz tugged on the lead rope and the mules fell into step. He rode down the creek, waving to the men he had come to know.

"Where you goin', Fritz?" Couts called.

"To find Davey Longworth."

"Watch yore topknot."

"You watch yours," Fritz returned, and then rode off to the west.

He was glad to be shut of Cherry Creek. He had not seen much good there. The place would probably never amount to much. He didn't care if he never saw it again.

Chapter Thirty-One

The snarling bear charged straight for Davey, and Sheila, who was pressed against the wall of the cave. Davey knew he would not be able to raise the barrel of his rifle and get off a shot before the grizzly reached him. Still, he tried, raising the barrel as he cocked the hammer back.

Eagle Heart leaped toward the bear, his knife drawn. The bear had not seen him, so he struck from behind, plunging the knife between the grizzly's shoulder blades. The bear roared, and they could hear the scrape of the blade against bone. It was a terrible sound that was quickly drowned out by the bear's angry roar. Blood spurted from its wound as it twisted its body, trying to claw at its back and dislodge the buried knife.

The bear shook, trying to throw its attacker off its back as Eagle Heart pulled downward on the knife with both hands. Slick with blood, his hands slipped off the handle and the bear twisted toward him. Now free of the Arapaho's weight, the furious animal roared and stood on its hind legs.

Eagle Heart started speaking to the bear in a series of grunts and Indian baby talk as the grizzly turned on him and fell to all fours.

"Come on, sister bear," Eagle Heart said in Arapaho, "come and let us dance."

Snarling, the bear lumbered toward the brave, who danced from side to side. Then the bear lunged, leaping up into the air until its forepaws were off the ground.

Davey brought his rifle to his shoulder and took aim at a spot just below where his companion's knife protruded from the dark furry back. He squeezed the trigger just as the grizzly was close to pouncing on Eagle Heart. The roar of the rifle was deafening inside the cave. White smoke belched out of the muzzle of the rifle and orange flame lit the cave walls for a brief moment.

Davey heard the ball thud into the bear's hide, but he could not see if Eagle Heart had gone down under the animal's onslaught.

The grizzly roared in pain, spun into the blazing fire, showering sparks like flung gold dust. As the wind fanned and cleared the smoke Davey laid down his rifle and drew his knife. The bear lunged at Eagle Heart, its coat smoking from smothered sparks caught in its fur. One paw slammed into the Arapaho's thigh and knocked the brave spinning against the cave wall.

Sheila stared at the angry and wounded bear in frozen fascination, voiceless with terror. Eagle Heart, dazed almost senseless, struggled to regain his footing as Davey charged at the bear's blind side. He drove his blade under the creature's armpit and twisted it, coring out a chunk of flesh the size of a billiard ball. Fresh blood oozed from the new wound and the grizzly roared even louder as it spun to face its latest attacker.

Davey ducked from a swipe of the bear's paw and danced to one side as it charged. Eagle Heart, shaking the cobwebs out of his head, rushed to grapple with the bear.

"No, Eagle Heart," Davey shouted, but it was too late. The bear lifted both arms to crush the Arapaho as he grabbed its neck and twisted it to one side. The bear embraced Eagle Heart even as the brave, using his own momentum, released his grip and fell away just before the massive arms closed around his body.

Davey was poised for another blow, and seeing an opening, he dashed toward the bear while its arms were close to its body. He slashed and slashed again at the exposed left arm of the bear and drew blood with each brutal swipe. The grizzly roared and, losing large amounts of blood, turned to attack him. Davey crouched and waited until the last second before he went in under the animal's arms and slashed it across its chest with a mighty rake of his hand.

Davey's knife opened a wound an eighth of an inch wide in the bear's chest and blood spilled over the crevice in crimson rivulets.

But the bear's right arm batted Davey as he went past and knocked him head over heels straight toward Sheila. She gasped and looked down, thinking the trapper was unconscious. Then, she saw the huge animal lumbering toward them to finish Davey off.

While this was going on Eagle Heart assumed a crouching position, then leaped toward the bear to cut off its rush toward the white man. Lowering his shoulder, the brave crashed into the animal's soft right side, the impact jarring his own shoulder until the pain shot needles through his brain and sent tortured shivers through his muscles.

But the force of his body was enough to knock the bear off its course and Davey was able to rise up in time to bat away one of its paws and drive his knife into the bear's right side near the gut. He pushed the knife deep and then tore downward toward the middle of the beast's belly. Sheila moved back against the wall, toward the cave entrance, ready to flee into the cold and snow.

Eyes wide with terror, she watched the bear as it fought desperately for its life, snarling and growling, roaring with rage. The animal saw Sheila move and suddenly whirled to give chase. Davey's heart lodged in his throat as he saw the bear shift its weight and drop again to all fours, then charge after Sheila.

"Run, Sheila," he cried, and leaped across the cave floor to intercept the grizzly. Eagle Heart, too, instantly understanding the situation, threw himself headlong at the bear's forepaws, as if oblivious to the danger to himself. Davey landed on the animal's back and tried to grab it around the neck. He hung on as the bear bucked in an effort to throw him off. Eagle Heart encircled one of the bear's forelegs and bit into it with his teeth. He bit deep and clamped his teeth in a hard grip.

In her desperation to escape, Sheila slipped on snow at the entrance and fell down, an unintentional act that may have saved her life. The bear stopped and bellowed in pain and rage, shaking its paw to throw Eagle Heart off its body. Davey took advantage of the animal's sudden stop and crawled up its back, holding on to its neck in a viselike grip with his left arm. He slipped his knife around the right side of the beast's neck and plunged the blade into the soft flesh clear to the hilt.

Then Davey pulled the knife blade toward him, opening up a broad slash in the bear's neck. Blood gushed from the wound as the grizzly crumpled, its vocal cords cut, its windpipe severed. Eagle Heart released his biting grip on the bear's leg and rolled away to avoid being crushed.

Davey's knife broke free and he tumbled from the bear's back, gasping for breath. Sheila turned and saw the dying creature inches from her legs; she curled up into a ball as she closed her eyes.

"She's done for," Davey breathed, exhaustion leaving him limp.

The bear huffed like a bellows and blood spurted with its every attempt at breathing. Its windpipe, white and bloody, dangled from the tear in its neck like a rubbery hose. Then its eyes began to glaze over with the frost-film of death and it whuffed the last of its breath from its lungs. The dying animal jerked with spasmodic convulsions as its brain, drained of blood, began to fail.

Eagle Heart looked at the bear's eyes and saw them close. Then its tongue snaked out of its mouth and hung limply over its teeth.

"Strong bear," the Indian said in English. "Brave bear. Good medicine."

"Good medicine," Davey echoed, still out of breath.

Still curled up in a ball, barely breathing, Sheila kept her eyes tightly shut.

"It's okay, Sheila," Davey said. "The bear's dead. You can get up now."

She opened her eyes and looked at the huge black corpse lying facedown, its tongue lolling from its mouth, its eyes shut. Its fur seemed to ripple in the firelight and she thought it was still alive.

"Are you sure it's dead?"

"Yes," Davey told her. "Get up, warm yourself by the fire."

Eagle Heart rose from the cave floor and walked to the bear. He grabbed his bloody knife and drew it from the animal's back. He wiped the blade on his buckskin leggings and then stooped to look at the corpse.

"Thank you, my sister," he said. "I will take your hide to warm my lodge and someday your children will eat the grasses that grow from my dead body and they will be warm and fat."

"What's he saying?" Sheila asked Davey as she stood by the fire, making sure that it was between her and the dead bear.

He told her that Eagle Heart was thanking the bear for giving up its life for them.

Sheila looked at him as if he were crazy. "The bear tried to kill him. Tried to kill us all. Why is he thanking it?"

"But we killed the bear—took its life. It is the Indian

way to thank the game whose lives they take and pray for forgiveness."

"That's an odd thing to do."

"Maybe, but the Arapaho believe in life. All life and for all time."

His prayer finished, Eagle Heart turned to Davey. He signed to him that he wanted to roll the bear over and skin it out.

"I will take the heart of this bear," the brave said in Arapaho. "It will make me strong."

"It was a very brave bear," Davey said in English.

"Yes," Eagle Heart agreed.

Together, the Arapaho and the white man pushed the bear onto its back. Eagle Heart made a deep cut around its neck, then down its body from neck to genitals. He began to slide the knife under its hide, separating the coat from the flesh. Sheila watched in fascination.

"Do you want me to help you?" Davey signed.

"No. Me take," Eagle Heart replied in English.

"I'll get more wood," Davey said, getting to his feet. He put wood on the fire and then left the cave.

"Make blanket," Eagle Heart said. "Make blanket for Sun Hair."

"I—I don't want it," Sheila said.

"Eagle Heart buy Sun Hair from Groot."

"No," Sheila said.

"Sun Hair make my heart full. I have good face for Sun Hair."

Sheila understood what he was saying, but she knew the Groots would never sell her to Eagle Heart. She looked at him in a new light, his copper skin glowing to a burnished smoothness in the glow from the fire as he deftly skinned the dead animal. He sliced open the grizzly's chest, and when he cut the arteries away from the heart and lifted it up to gaze at it, she turned away. When she looked back, Eagle Heart was eating the bear's heart raw.

Dizzy, she took a deep breath to keep from fainting. The Arapaho's mouth and chin were covered with blood. He looked, then, like a savage, and she shuddered.

She wondered if she could ever live with such a man, share his bed, bear him children. She shook off the thought, but couldn't deny that she was curious about Eagle Heart.

And she knew he was in love with her. And then she had a most surprising thought that made her ashamed of herself.

Sheila almost hoped Davey would not come back from his hunt for wood.

Chapter
Thirty-Two

Peaches felt the icy-cold winds blow down on the plains from the Rocky Mountains as he rode slowly up the South Platte. He pulled his coat tighter around him and ducked his head so that the winds did not burn his face. His beaver hat was already flecked with snowflakes and his horse's mane was dusted with white powder.

The sky was dark and forbidding, with clouds scudding down from the mountains, their underbellies black as a potbelly stove. He rode into the brunt of the wind from the northwest and wondered where he would find shelter on the deserted prairie.

Every time he looked straight ahead, snow blew into his eyes, blinding him. He shivered and knew he would not last long without shelter and warmth from a blazing fire. But there was no sign of any habitation. He debated whether to cross the river and climb into the mountains, where at least he could build a fire and put some kind of a temporary shelter together. From the looks of the sky and the whip of the chill wind, he knew this was no passing storm, but a two- or three-day blow at least. By afternoon, the plain would be covered with a half foot of snow.

He had long ago lost Cleel's tracks, but he knew the general direction in which the renegade had headed, and the

South Platte was a good enough guide. Surely he would be able to recognize any place that Cleel had veered off, but he strongly suspected the man he followed would not stray far from water. Three horses would leave a lot of tracks since the snowfall was still light. While the snow covered the tracks with a smooth blanket, if Cleel turned off, Peaches reasoned, they would still leave some sign.

The snowfall began to increase, the wind now piling it up in drifts, and the temperature continued to drop. Still, Peaches kept looking up at the foothills across the river, trying to locate some likely fords in the swift-running current. He was not yet ready to give up and seek shelter in the mountains, but if the storm got any worse, he knew he would have no choice.

He had spent too much time getting down out of the mountains, and along the rough trail Cleel had chosen, he had spent too much time backtracking, guessing wrong, losing the track and finding it again. Cleel now had covered a much greater distance than Peaches had in a shorter period of time. Peaches cursed himself, the weather, and everything on earth he could think of as his mind wandered, drifting like the snow blowing around him.

Suddenly he heard a soft sound and stopped, listening. He looked around, but the snow was blowing and swirling and he could see nothing. It had sounded like a horse whickering and it was clear to him that his own horse had heard it, too, for his ears were now twisting, stiffened to inverted cones.

The former trapper waited, but the sound did not come again.

He could still see the foothills, but the mountains beyond were shrouded in a snowy haze and he knew that they would soon disappear altogether. He could no longer make out the snowcaps at all.

At that moment a snowy tumbleweed blew across the

plain, uprooted from the bank of the South Platte, where it had landed a few days before. As it brushed across the earth Peaches saw a maze of rabbit tracks and the cloven prints of antelope, but not a sign of a horseshoe print among any of them.

The veil of mist that hung over the mountain peaks slowly descended and Peaches felt isolated and alone, the kind of alone that bred panic in lesser men. His eyelashes caught and held the snowflakes, and when he batted them, they melted on his cheeks or began to glaze over with the cold.

For a while now Peaches had begun to suspect that he was being followed. But when he looked around, he saw no one. Yet he couldn't shake that feeling of eyes staring at the back of his head, or of a presence somewhere close by, and he kept looking at his shadow, faint as it was, to see if that might be what was giving him the willies.

He stopped several times and waited, listening. But he heard nothing except the silent tink of the snow falling and was beginning to doubt that his senses even detected any sound at all.

"Get a grip on yourself, Beecham," he said aloud, and the ensuing silence only served to make him feel even more alone.

As he listened to the howling wind, Peaches could have sworn he heard someone crying, or screaming, but he decided that it was only a trick of the senses, something in his imagination. Still, he felt a shivering inside that had nothing to do with the cold.

Turning in the saddle, he looked toward his backtrail, but saw nothing. He scanned as far as his vision would reach and he thought he saw a shape, something darker than the snowy landscape, but he could not be sure.

"Who's there?" he called.

Then he stopped, because he thought he heard an answer. He waited, listening.

"Is somebody out there?" he called, then touched the stock of his rifle in its sheath, ready to pull it from the scabbard. "Hooooo," he called.

"Hoooooo," he heard in reply.

"Over here," Peaches called.

"Wait," the voice called, a voice shredded by the wind and muffled by the falling snow.

"Come on," the former trapper yelled. "Hurry."

Sitting still like that made Peaches feel even colder and he wished that whoever it was who was calling to him would ride up and turn out to be a friend. White man or Indian? He did not know, but he suspected it was someone who spoke English, who understood him.

"Where are you?" he called.

"I'm coming."

And Peaches thought he recognized the voice. It had just a trace of a German accent.

"Who are you?" he called, hope growing stronger in his heart, and then he saw the dark shape grow larger, horse and man, both dusted with snow.

"Peaches, is that you?"

"Fritz?"

"Yeah, it is Fritz. What are you doing way out here?"

The trapper came close enough for Peaches to make out his face and confirm that the rider was indeed Fritz Stamm.

"I could ask you the same question, Fritz. I thought you were still back at Cherry Creek."

Fritz rode up close, out of breath. His horse's legs were covered with snow, past the knees, so Peaches knew that they had ridden through some heavy drifts.

"Everything went to hell back there, Peaches, I tell you."

"Well, everything went to hell up in the mountains with Cleel. Any of the bunch get back?"

"Only one. Cox. He had a big story to tell about John Cleel, by God."

"So do I, the bastard."

"It is hard to figure such a man doing those things, robbing his own kind." Fritz eyed the other man suspiciously.

"Well, he by God sure as hell did it. Are you tracking him?"

"No," Fritz said. "I'm goin' to look for Davey. You seen him?"

Peaches shook his head. "Never expected to. I'm atrackin' Cleel."

"Cleel's out here? Where's he goin'?"

"Damned if I know," Peaches said. "I lost his track an hour or so ago, anyways."

"Davey said there was some settlers out this away," Fritz said.

"Hmm."

"Homesteadin' right along the Platte."

"It would be a blessing if we come up on 'em," Peaches said.

"We got to go where the Poudre comes into the Platte."

"That shouldn't be far," Peaches reasoned, "but I've lost all track of distance."

"Just keep the river on your left hand and we'll come acrost them settlers."

So the two men set out from that meeting place and followed the South Platte north, its leaden waters running full, whitecapped from the blistering wind, snowflakes melting as they struck the agitated waters.

Fritz kept his thoughts to himself. He was wary of the man who had tried to kill Davey, but trouble and the weather had forced them together. He'd just have to be careful till they parted company.

"I smell smoke," Fritz said, after he and Peaches had ridden north for an hour.

The trapper-turned-prospector sniffed the wind. "I don't catch it."

"There," Fritz said as the wind gusted, swirling across a drift that sent flakes spiraling upward in a miniature whirlwind.

"I got it now. Wood smoke."

"Damned sure."

"Can you make out a soddy?"

Fritz peered into the funnel of snow that blanked out all physical features on the prairie. "Nope. We got to stay sharp and keep our eyes peeled."

"That we do," Peaches agreed.

The freak snowstorm continued to blanket the land as the two trappers forged ahead like white ghosts into the brunt of the wind. They could barely see and the cold was seeping into their coats and snicking at their flesh like probing icicles seeking the last remaining pockets of warmth.

Soon the blasting wind paused, as if the earth was taking a breath, and through the vortex of whiteness, Fritz was able to discern a dark shape perhaps fifty yards ahead. Then he saw the orange glow of lantern light shining through a window before the wind picked up again and closed off the vision.

"Somep'n ahead," Fritz said.

"What?"

"A house. Light."

"I can't see a damned thing," Peaches confessed. "I think I've gone snow-blind."

"Look off yonder, to the left. That be the Poudre roarin' into the Platte."

Through the swirl of snow Peaches caught a glimpse of the Cache de la Poudre as it raged into the South Platte, its rocking waves flecked with whitecaps.

"I see it," he said.

"Now look to the right, up where the land rises to that knoll."

Peaches swung his gaze to the right and made out that

the land did indeed rise, but he could not judge depth or distance and could not tell if there was a knoll there or not. Then, as the wind eased again, he saw what Fritz had seen, the dark outline of a house or fort and the glow of lantern light, strangely incongruous in the snowy emptiness where everything was pure white, without definition.

"That must be the settlers' place," Fritz said.

"It ain't no tepee."

The two men turned their horses toward the dark shape and saw its outlines become more defined as they drew closer. Lamplight glowed in the windows like beacons in a wilderness of white.

"Hello the house," Peaches called as he and Fritz stopped in front of the porch.

"Louder," Fritz told him.

Peaches called out again. A curtain moved at the window and a man's face appeared, his features shadowed by the lamp at his back. A second later a rifle barrel stuck out a gun port below the window.

"We're friendly," Fritz called in a loud voice.

"Go away." The man's voice was gruff.

"We're cold," Peaches said. "We mean no harm."

"I don't know you."

"We're friends of Davey Longworth," Fritz yelled as the snow whipped up around them from a sudden gust that stirred up the snow on the roof of the house.

Loud voices spoke up inside the house, arguing, Fritz was sure. Presently the front door opened and a large young man appeared, holding a rifle pointed at the trappers.

"You can't come in," Kris said. "We don't take to strangers."

"Mister, we're damned near freezing and we're lookin' for shelter."

"Not here," Kris said.

"This is the only place around," Peaches called. "You ain't gonna turn a man away in such a storm, are you?"

Kris hesitated for a moment, then the door closed. More loud voices, one a woman's. Two men, Fritz figured.

At last the door opened again, and a large man stood in its frame. He, too, held a rifle in his hands, and it was pointed at the two men.

"Go away," Hans said. "We have no room for you."

"Mister, you're either a fool or all bad," Peaches returned. "It's freezing out here and you've got shelter. All we want is someplace to bed down until the storm passes."

"There's a lean-to at the side of the house. You can go there."

Peaches started to say something else, but Hans turned and slammed the door behind him as he entered the house.

"What the hell." Peaches turned to Fritz. "The bastards."

"We'll look at the lean-to," the trapper said, and rode to the side of the house. There, they saw a small shelter, board and batten with a tarp tacked to it. It didn't look large enough to house two men. Peaches climbed down from his horse and looked inside. It was dark. Some bedding lay rumpled on its bottom; he could feel it with his hands. It was cold inside.

"We'll freeze to death in there," Peaches said as he came back to his horse.

"What can we do?" Fritz asked.

"We can break into that house," Peaches answered. "At gunpoint. At least we won't freeze."

It seemed like a reasonable plan, but then they heard a noise, and when they turned around, Hans and Kris stood there with guns pointed at them.

"If you try to break in, we'll kill you," Kris threatened.

"Maybe we kill them anyway," Hans said.

The two men heard the click as father and son cocked

their rifles. The wind howled and blowing snow swept down on the two settlers holding them at gunpoint.

Then the younger of the two raised his rifle, pointing it straight at Fritz, while his father brought his rifle up and aimed it at Peaches. The wind dropped off suddenly and it became very quiet.

Chapter Thirty-Three

Davey knew he had made a mistake the moment his foot touched the ground. He felt his foot sink and knew he must have stepped on a ledge that he had been unable to see in the dark of the snowstorm. His arms were laden with firewood, and when the edge of the ledge gave way, he struggled to maintain his balance, already realizing that he had no way to regain his footing.

He heard the ghastly sound of the rock breaking up, the talus sliding down a slope and taking him with it in a miniature avalanche. The wood in his arms went flying and he suddenly found himself plummeting down the slope as the sliding rocks roared in his ears.

Davey hit the slope midway down with a jarring thud. Pain shot through his elbows and backside. He tried to dig in his heels to slow his downward momentum. As he did so a small tree growing from the sidehill lashed him across the face, leaving raw welts on his cheeks. One of his heels struck a rock and he felt pain shoot up through his leg to the kneecap. He twisted sideways and found himself sliding on his side. Pain shot through his ribs, but at least he could feel himself beginning to slow. He twisted some more until he was on his belly, then clawed at the slope with his bare hands, fingers plunging through fresh snow.

Davey skidded down the slope slicked by the snowfall, his hands clawing at bushes, rocks, his toes digging in to slow him, but whatever he did, he kept sliding, sliding, until he dropped off still another slope and plunged into a deep ravine, his fall cushioned by pine and spruce boughs.

He heard the snap of tree limbs as he fell, and then he hit bottom, landing in a crevice in which he became wedged as snow and rock continued to fall on him, covering him with a dome of material that rested on outstretched boughs.

Then the slide ceased and Davey lay there in the darkness, unable to move, but alive at least. He looked up and saw that he had been protected by close-growing trees whose boughs formed a canopy over him. The weight of snow and rock pressed the branches down, but there was room to breathe. He tried to push himself up, but was wedged in too tight. Exhausted, he lay back and listened to the falling snow, wondering if the boughs would break and either start another slide or crush him to death with the weight of their burden. His back hurt, and he was scratched from head to toe, but he could tell that he wasn't bleeding profusely from any of his injuries.

"Damn," he said, wondering how he was going to get out from between the two boulders, and if this place was going to be his grave.

"I wonder where Davey is," Sheila said as she threw another piece of wood on the fire.

"No savvy," Eagle Heart said. His words were lost on Sheila, who was unfamiliar with the slang learned from the Mexicans.

The Arapaho was patiently skinning out the dead grizzly, intent on obtaining a robe and food. Sheila kept looking at the cave entrance, expecting the trapper to come walking into the cave at any moment, his arms laden with fresh firewood.

Finally she walked away from the fire and squatted near Eagle Heart, who did not look up from his skinning.

"We should look for Davey," she stated.

Eagle Heart looked up at her. "Look?"

"For Davey."

"Davey come soon."

Sheila shook her head. "He must have gotten lost."

The Indian's eyebrows arched. "Him no lost."

"You understand me," she said.

"Me savvy."

Sheila looked at the cave entrance. Snow was swirling outside and drifting into the cave. She had never seen such emptiness before, never heard such a silence.

Eagle Heart carefully pulled the bear's coat from its back and rolled it up, set it against a wall of the cave. Then he began to cut the meat into slices and sections. He laid these inside the stomach cavity. He sharpened two sticks and skewered two pieces of meat onto the pointed ends. Handed Sheila one of the sticks.

"'Cook," he said. "Eat." He rubbed his belly with one hand and made gestures of putting food into his mouth. Sheila nodded and took one of the sticks. Eagle Heart poked his stick into the fire and she did the same. Soon the smell of roasting bear filled the cave. Sheila's stomach roiled with hunger. She looked at the cave entrance again, saw that the clouds and snow still made the day dark, almost like night, and wondered what had happened to Davey.

As the two remaining residents of the cave chewed the cooked bear meat in silence, Sheila kept hoping Davey would come back, but time wore on and there was no sign of him. She began to realize that something bad must have befallen him.

"Much snow," Eagle Heart said when they were finished eating.

"Where is Davey?" she asked.

Eagle Heart shrugged. "No savvy," he replied.

"Aren't you going to look for him?"

The Arapaho looked puzzled.

"Look for him." Sheila shaded her eyes and moved her head as if she were searching for something.

Eagle Heart grinned with understanding. He made sign and spoke in broken English. "No track. Much snow. Wait for sun. Find Davey."

Then Sheila began to cry softly. Eagle Heart put another chunk of wood on the fire and moved over to her. He held her face in his hands and looked into her eyes.

"Sun Hair no cry. No bring Davey."

Sheila broke down then, and crumpled into the Arapaho leader's arms. She sobbed until her tears dried up, but found comfort in Eagle Heart's strong embrace.

"Good woman," he commented. "Brave heart."

"No," Sheila said, her voice weak from crying. "I'm scared and worried about Davey."

"Davey come soon," Eagle Heart told her, but the conviction in his voice sounded false to her ears.

Finally she pulled gently away from Eagle Heart and looked at him closely. She had felt so safe in his arms. She wondered if it was only an illusion. "You are good, too, Eagle Heart," she said.

"Eagle Heart good," he repeated. "Heap good."

Sheila laughed and went to him again, snuggling into his arms. "Take care of me," she said.

Eagle Heart seemed not to understand what she had said, but he held her more tightly. Sheila, facing the cave entrance, watched the snow fall steadily and listened to the wind keen as it twisted in and out of the cave. The snowfall was mesmerizing, and she felt her eyelids growing heavy. Soon she fell asleep. The warmth of the fire and the tender way that Eagle Heart held her made her feel secure and content.

Once he knew she was asleep, Eagle Heart gently laid

her down and rose to add wood to the fire. Then he carried the girl to Davey's bedroll and laid her atop it, covering her with Davey's saddle blanket. As she slept he scraped the bear hide with his knife, removing fat and flesh until the inside was smooth and clean. Then he laid the hide out near the fire, fur down, to let it dry.

That done, he got up and walked out of the cave. The snow was still falling and he could see no signs of clearing in the sky. He listened for a long time, looking into the snow, sometimes at individual flakes. He sang a silent song to the Great Spirit, marveling at the wonders of all nature, of all things, and all beings. He gave thanks for being alive on that day, and for the Sun-haired white woman that had come into his life.

When he finished his prayer, the Arapaho brave turned and walked back to the fire. He got tobacco from his pouch and offered it to the four directions before throwing the leaves on the fire. Then he put more wood on the fire and went to the spot where Sheila lay sleeping. He lay down beside her and closed his eyes. The white woman did not stir. Before he went to sleep, he thought of the bear and of its great brave heart and was glad that he had eaten it. He felt full in his belly and he felt that his life was full. Soon it would fill up even more when he bought the Sun-haired white woman from her master, Groot.

"Life is good," Eagle Heart whispered before he dropped off to sleep.

By morning the snow had stopped falling. The skies were still overcast, but a fresh breeze was blowing up from the south and Eagle Heart knew the skies would clear. The sun would rise and go across the sky and melt the snow.

"Something must have happened to Davey," Sheila began again. She had awakened that morning to find Eagle Heart sleeping next to her. She closed her eyes and waited until he awoke, too ashamed to speak to him. Now she stood beside him outside the cave, content that they had eaten more bear meat and that the cave had stayed warm.

Eagle Heart only grunted. Then he signed to her that he would look for the trapper.

"I will go with you," Sheila offered, and they set out, walking along the ledge until they stepped onto grass covered with snow. There were tracks of deer and elk in the snow, but none made by a man. Eagle Heart covered both sides of the cave, but they never found any sign of Davey.

"We go," the Arapaho said. "Go home."

"But what about Davey?"

"Davey dead maybe."

"No, he can't be. . . ."

"We go," Eagle Heart said again, and took her hand. She followed him in a daze back to the cave, helped him pack the bear meat and hide on one of Davey's mules. Then she watched as the brave did what seemed to her a strange thing. He packed Davey's bedroll on the trapper's horse, led him to a grassy place, scraped the snow away so the horse could feed, and tied him to a tree with a long rope.

"Why are you doing that?" she asked.

"Maybe Davey come."

And Eagle Heart left one of the pack mules there, too, tethering them in other places where they could graze. Then she and Eagle Heart rode on his horse down to the place of the skulls and continued down the Cache de la Poudre.

As they rode off, Sheila wished she had called out to Davey at least once while she and Eagle Heart were looking for him, but she had not. She believed now, in her heart, that Davey was dead.

And that thought made her very sad, but she did not cry. She just squeezed her arms around Eagle Heart's waist and it seemed she could hear her heart pounding against his buckskinned back.

She looked back once to see if Davey was following them, but she saw only the snowy mountains and the jays flitting from tree to tree, knocking off clumps of snow each time they alit or took off. The mountains seemed like a giant tombstone atop Davey's grave.

Chapter
Thirty-Four

Their weapons aimed at the strangers, Hans and Kris turned in the direction of the sudden noise. Fritz's jaw dropped and his mouth opened in surprise. Peaches stared at the stout woman with the rifle and thought he must be addled, for her eyes were blazing and she swung the rifle as if she was about to shoot any or all of them.

"Let them come into the house, Hans," Maddy said, firmly. "We are not animals."

"Maddy, put down the gun," Hans told her.

"Hans, these two men will freeze to death out here. We need to show some kindness."

"Strangers," Hans muttered. Then he turned to Peaches and Fritz. "Give the boy your rifles and you can come inside. But you must go when I tell you to."

"That's good enough for us, mister," Peaches agreed.

Kris took their rifles and removed the flints.

"You can put up your horses in the barn," Maddy said. "If you can find it in this storm."

Hans pointed toward the barn, invisible in the blowing snow. "Over there," he said.

"Much obliged." Fritz never meant words more truly.

"We're mighty grateful," Peaches added.

"Kris, you go with them," Hans told his son. "If they try to steal anything, you shoot them."

"Yes, Papa," Kris mumbled obediently.

"We ain't thieves," Peaches put in.

"Hurry up." Hans waved them off. "We are cold out here, too."

Peaches said nothing. He and Fritz led their horses to the barn, which emerged out of the darkness and snowfall. Both were aware that Kris held a loaded rifle on them, so they moved slowly.

"It's small, this barn," Fritz observed.

"Open the door and let's get these horses inside."

Fritz raised the crossbar and opened the single barn door, then walked into the pitch-black interior. He heard a mule bray softly and a horse nicker. There were no stalls, just an open space. He felt for a post or stanchion.

"Don't unsaddle 'em," Kris said as Peaches entered the barn. "You won't be here that long."

"Any grain or hay?" Fritz asked. "We'll pay for it."

"You can pay us first and then give your horses some cracked corn and hay," Kris replied. He waited outside, listened to the rustle of straw, the creak of leather. But neither trapper spoke. In a few minutes both men emerged from the barn.

"You can go to the house now," Kris told them sullenly.

"Mighty fine welcome," Peaches grumbled.

"Yah," Fritz agreed, reverting to his German accent, "welcome at gunpoint."

"You shut up," Kris ordered, the sullenness suddenly leaving his voice as he realized that he was in authority, and liked it.

The two trappers walked around to the front of the house and up the steps. Maddy opened the door for them.

She no longer carried a rifle, but they could see it leaning against the wall just inside the door.

"Go to the kitchen," she said. "Where the lantern is shining."

Peaches walked past the front room and turned left at a hall that led to the kitchen. He noticed the sparse furnishings, the gun ports in the walls, all of them filled with quick-pull wooden dowels to keep out the wintry air.

When they got to the kitchen, Hans was waiting for them, holding the rifle so that it was pointed at the two men. "Sit," he said.

Peaches and Fritz took chairs and quickly sat down. Kris eyed the two men warily, then shot a questioning look at his father.

"Kris, you wait in the other room. Watch the door. Look from the window every few minutes, eh?"

"Yes, Papa," Kris answered dutifully.

As the young man lumbered off, Peaches sniffed the kitchen air with its heady aroma of coffee . . . and something else. He looked at Fritz, who, obviously, was also smelling the same aromas.

"Hot apple cider," Peaches commented.

"We have coffee for you," Maddy said, setting three tin cups on the home-built table. She set a fourth cup on the counter for herself, then poured coffee in the cups, handed one to Hans, who sat near the doorway, a small butcher table next to him, against the wall. Pots and pans hung from wooden dowels set in the logs of the kitchen, which was neat and spotless.

"Mighty nice of you, ma'am," Peaches said, lifting his cup to his lips. Steam coiled from the dark surface, suffusing the air with its aroma. Another pot stood on the small woodstove, sending forth vapors of apple cider.

"Now maybe you boys can tell me what you're doing

out here," Hans began, after tasting from his cup. "And your names as well."

"Beecham," Peaches said. "They call me Peaches."

"I'm Fritz Stamm. Davey Longworth told me about you."

"And you?" Hans glared at Peaches as he spoke.

"I'm alookin' for a man."

"What man?"

"He calls hisself John Cleel."

Hans and Maddy exchanged a look that was not lost on the former trapper.

"You know Cleel?" Peaches asked.

"We know him," Hans said tightly. "Are you a friend of John Cleel?"

Peaches shook his head. "No. He ain't no friend of mine."

"So why are you looking for him?" Maddy asked, edging nearer to the table.

Peaches looked at Fritz. Fritz nodded.

"Well, ma'am, this Cleel done robbed a bunch of prospectors and trappers, some who was friends of mine. He kilt my friend Tom."

"So you do not like this Cleel," Hans concluded.

"No. I aim to kill him when I find him."

"He was here," Maddy blurted out. Hans gave her a sharp look.

"He was here?" Peaches' surprise was clear in his voice. "When?"

"A few days ago," Maddy replied. "He said he would be back."

"Where did he go?"

"To the east. I think he was going to see the other settlers he brought out here." Maddy did not look at her husband while she spoke.

"You cannot wait for him here," Hans said.

"No. I'll go after him when the storm quits," Peaches said.

"And you, what do you want with Davey?" Hans asked Fritz.

"I have some bad news for him."

"Bad news?" Maddy asked, her curiosity piqued.

"The fur market done dropped to zero," Fritz explained. "He was acomin' after his cache up the Poudre."

"Yes, he went there," Hans said, giving Maddy a warning look to say no more.

"Say, didn't you have a girl with you?" Fritz asked.

"She is not here," Hans said.

Fritz and Peaches exchanged looks, but neither spoke. They drank their coffee in silence, began to shed their heavy coats, which had dripped on the floor. Maddy wiped up the moisture, but did not offer to take their coats, which they hung on the backs of their chairs.

"How long do you think this storm will last?" Hans asked after a while.

"Be over by morning, I reckon," Fritz said.

Peaches nodded.

"Then, you will be on your way," Hans told him coldly.

Both Peaches and Fritz nodded.

Just then there was a commotion in the front room. They all heard a chair scrape and something bang against the wall and then heavy footsteps approaching the kitchen. Hans brought his rifle up as Peaches and Fritz started to rise from their chairs.

"Do not move," the settler ordered.

A moment later Kris burst into the room, his eyes flashing a wildness, his face pale.

"What is it?" Maddy cried.

"Somebody's comin'," Kris said. "Carrying torches, riding in from the east. A lot of men, I think."

Maddy looked at Hans. "Who could it be?"

"I don't know," Hans said, "but we find out soon, eh? You two just sit there. Watch them, Kris. I will go to the window and look out."

With that, Hans left the room. Kris sat down, his eyes fixed on the two men as he nervously tapped one foot on the floor. Maddy remained standing, almost transfixed as she listened for sounds from the front of the house.

"Who you reckon would be out riding in weather like this?" Peaches asked, looking at Fritz.

Fritz shrugged. "Fools," was all he answered.

At that moment the front door creaked open. Those in the kitchen all heard footsteps. Then the door slammed shut. Kris and Maddy both jerked involuntarily.

A few seconds later all in the kitchen could hear loud voices outside. Then the front door opened again and they could hear Hans shouting.

"Quick, Maddy, Kris, all of you, come outside."

Kris stood there motionless as Maddy started to walk from the kitchen. "Come on," she said. "Hans said all of us."

In their haste to comply, Peaches and Fritz beat Kris out of the kitchen. As they walked outside, Maddy and Kris caught up with them in ungainly strides.

In front of the house they saw a group of men sitting on horses, bundled against the wind and snow with scarves pulled up to their faces, all holding torches blazing with oil-wrapped rags. It was an eerie sight. Orange light painted the snow and illuminated the falling flakes into tiny bright suns.

"Who—who?" Maddy screeched.

"Our friends," Hans said, "from the settlement to the east. They have brought word of John Cleel."

Peaches grabbed Fritz's arm and squeezed it. Fritz stared at the assembled men, who, with their faces covered, looked like brigands.

Rifles jutted from snow-dusted scabbards and the horses

blew white steam into the air. Fritz had never seen a sight like it and was at a total loss for words. For a long moment no one said anything, staring at the men on horseback. They looked like frozen ghosts in the flickering light of the torches.

"Listen to what they have to say, Maddy," Hans said finally. Then, to one of the men: "Jan, tell us about John Cleel and what he did to all of you."

Chapter
Thirty-Five

D avey lay on his back, his stomach roiling with hunger. But the snow-laden boughs that pressed down on him had kept him warm during the night. He had slept and lived to open his eyes with the first feeble rays of the morning sun. The snow had stopped falling and he knew he must try to unwedge himself from the rocks that held him prisoner.

He could not see much, but the sky was blue, with only traces of scattered and tattered clouds. He blinked the sleep from his eyes and moved his hands down along his sides. The rocks were cold to the touch and it took an effort to hold his palms fast to the surface of the snow covering the boulders on which he lay.

He pushed hard and lifted his backside, straining to lift his body free of the two rocks. That was when Davey discovered that he had no feeling in his buttocks. They were numb from the cold. He relaxed and began to move his body, undulating his hips slightly, mentally forcing the muscles to squeeze and unsqueeze.

As blood rushed to the chilled extremities he began to feel sharp pains in his rear. Then he tried lifting himself again, and this time he could feel movement. He knew he had to decide which way to roll out of the rocks. If he made the wrong choice, he could either wedge himself in tighter or perhaps start a landslide that might dash him against trees or rocks farther down the slope.

Davey rested for a spell, took a deep breath to clear his mind. He tried to picture his position between the boulders. He carefully moved his head from left to right, trying to determine the type of terrain around where he lay.

There were bushes, small trees on either side of him. He could not see downward, past his feet. He knew he had to trust to luck and perhaps his limited dexterity. But he had worked the traps in frozen waters and knew how to keep his fingers from freezing.

As he lay there he began to flex his hands and digits, closing and unclosing them to restore warm circulation. The pain began to seep into the thawing joints and he felt a mild sense of relief.

He relaxed and thought over his situation. If he did not break free of the rocks that held him tight, he would die of hunger and thirst. Already, his mouth was dry and his stomach felt the gnaw of an unsatisfied appetite.

Determined to be free, Davey twisted once more toward his left side, and to his surprise, he was able to turn away from the rock on his right side. Controlling the rush of elation, he hunched up and his belly cleared the rock on the left. Pushing higher he was able to swing his right leg out until it touched ground. Next, he slid sideways and pushed off on the boulder. He felt his right foot slide and then he slid a few yards until he was stopped by a scrub juniper bush. He lay there for a few seconds wondering at how easy it had been once he had relaxed and tried a different tack.

Slowly, carefully, Davey stood up. He was wobbly and weak, but as he came upright, he began to feel his strength return. He looked up the snowy slope and saw where he had slid the night before. The place had drifted with snow, but he knew the location of the cave, even though he could not see it from his position.

Davey stepped to more solid footing and stomped his feet, knocking off some of the snow that clung to his boots. As feeling began to return to his toes he slapped his arms against his sides, brushed snow from his back, his leggings. Then he walked on an angle up the slope, flexing his cold fingers.

Breathless, he reached the rimrock, caught sight of the cave, or at least a portion of it, off to his left.

"Sheila," he called. "Eagle Heart."

His voice bounced off the rocks in pealing echoes, followed by hollow silence. He felt like he was the only human on earth, and a deep sense of loneliness swept through him.

He continued to climb up to the rimrock, and when he reached it, he called out again to Sheila and Eagle Heart. But, as before, there was no answer.

Davey entered the cave and saw the remains of the grizzly, his bedroll neatly rolled up, the fire smothered in dirt. In the cold dank air, he shivered and again felt a mantle of deep loneliness settle over him. Picking up his bedroll, he returned outside and breathed deeply of the crisp mountain air.

When, unexpectedly, he heard a whinny, his heart seemed to leap inside his chest, and he hurried as much as his weakened condition would allow to the rimrock away from the cave. Climbing up to the place where he and Eagle Heart had tethered the horses and mules, he saw his horse pawing the snow.

All alone.

Davey looked around, heard a noise in the timber. A quick movement and he saw one of his mules. Just one of them. He scanned all around the flat and did not see the other mule. He began to study the tracks, and after a few moments he knew what had happened. Eagle Heart had taken one of his mules, packed the bear meat and skin on its back, and, as revealed by the deep set of pony tracks, had ridden with Sheila out of the meadow.

Davey found his saddle and a pannier, bridled his horse, and brought the mule out of the trees. He saddled his horse and mounted up, picking up the mule's lead. He checked his powder and put fresh fine grains of primer in the pan.

Now he was ready to follow Eagle Heart's tracks off the plateau. It was early afternoon and the Arapaho had a good start on him. But at least the storm was over and the sky again blue, the clouds small and fluffy. The loneliness he had felt before had dissipated, but something else gnawed at him, and it was more than just hunger and thirst.

Sheila. She had gone off with Eagle Heart. They had been alone all night. He caught himself wondering if the girl had fallen in love with the Arapaho. He knew that Eagle Heart wanted her for his wife. Had the two come to some agreement? They had ridden off together, probably left him for dead. Why hadn't they waited and looked for him?

These questions bothered Davey as he rode slowly down slippery slopes and over hidden game trails. Eagle Heart had left his dun gelding and one mule, his rifle and bedroll. Why? If the Indian and Sheila thought he was dead, why leave those things? And if they didn't think he was dead, why hadn't they looked for him?

His thoughts kept going in circles, coming back to the beginning with each one. There was no way that Eagle Heart or Sheila could have known what had happened to him, but it seemed that neither had bothered to find out.

Davey was not angry, but he was puzzled. And he was confused. He had not faced his own feelings about Sheila, but he was certain that he liked her, and more than that, admired her, for her courage and her spunk.

The ride back was treacherous and he saw places where Eagle Heart's pony had skidded and foundered in drifts. When he reached the place of the skulls, he wondered if he should retrieve part of his fur cache. He could not get it all with only one mule. He stopped, took out his pipe, and filled it with tobacco. He used the glass to light it from the rays of the high sun. He smoked and he thought, and he still asked himself the same persistent questions.

The snow was melting fast and the Poudre raged with the runoff. Davey surveyed his situation, and from the looks of the river, he knew he would have a hard time crossing the Platte later on. It could be days before the rivers settled down enough to enable a fording.

Hunger pangs seized his stomach. He climbed out of the saddle and drank from the edge of the river, which only made him hungrier. He thought of the cache and decided against retrieving any of the furs. He had cooking utensils in his saddlebags and there should be game aplenty on the move after the storm. It took him only a few minutes to decide to leave the cache intact and set up camp. There was no cause to hurry now. He could not change the course of nature; he could not bring the rivers down any quicker.

Davey led his horse and mule into the timber and found a suitable place to wait out the days. He set up camp and took his rifle and went looking for deer or any other suitable game.

As he hunted he thought of Sheila and Eagle Heart, where they might be. Would they, too, have to wait for the South Platte to subside before they crossed over to the prairie? Or would Eagle Heart know an Indian way to cross above the confluence of the Poudre and Platte?

Those questions were forgotten when he saw fresh deer tracks a half mile from his camp. He followed the spoor for a few hundred yards and then stopped up short, realizing he was not the only one hunting the deer. A fresh set of moccasin prints were joined to the cloven prints of the deer. And the tracks had clearly been made by a Ute brave.

Suddenly the woods were very still and Davey knew that he was in danger.

Chapter
Thirty-Six

Peaches looked down on the group of men who had ridden in from the eastern prairie settlement. Men whose names or faces he did not know, but who had information about the man he was hunting, John Cleel.

"What's this about Cleel?" he asked.

Jan Van Dorn, the man who looked to be the leader, stared at Peaches, held his torch up higher so that he could see the trapper's face.

"You know him?"

"I know him as a murderer and a thief."

"He came to us as a trader," Jan said. "We had known him in St. Louis. He told us about the land out here in Jefferson Territory."

"That is right." Hans nodded. "Go on, Jan. Tell us what Cleel did to you."

"We're freezing out here," said one of the homesteaders. "Can't we build a fire or come inside?"

"There is little room inside for all of you," Maddy said. "Perhaps we could build a fire outside and I could bring you coffee."

"Kris, fetch some wood for a fire," Hans told his son. "We will build it with their torches in front of our home."

The homesteaders murmured their approval and started

to clear a space in the snow for a fire. Two of them accompanied Kris to bring firewood.

Peaches walked down the steps off the porch and sought out Jan.

"Is Cleel alive?" he asked.

"Yes, the bastard is alive and I wish he were dead and in his grave."

"He will be," Peaches assured him.

"Bring the chairs, Hans," Maddy said to her husband, flushed with excitement. Soon Kris and the others returned with the wood, which they laid down in the cleared circle, then the settlers set torches to the pile. The fire was blazing by the time Hans brought chairs he had made from inside the house. Others sat on logs, or saddles, rubbing their hands in the warmth of the blaze.

"I will fix a big stew," Maddy announced, smiling, "and we have cider and coffee. Kris, you come and help me."

"Aw, Ma," Kris complained.

"Come along now. There will be time later to enjoy the company of our friends."

Kris grumbled, but followed his mother into the cabin. It appeared he, too, was glad to see friends they had made in Missouri again. Men lit pipes and cut off chunks of tobacco from twists, stuck the wads in their mouths.

"You say Cleel sold you his goods?" Hans asked.

Jan Van Dorn nodded. "They were used rifles and pistols and they were cheap."

"They were stolen from dead men," Peaches informed the group. He and Fritz were standing outside the circle. Heads turned in their direction.

"Ah, I suspected as much," said a man named Dieter. "I never did trust John Cleel. He was not a man who kept his word."

Several men nodded in agreement.

"That was not the worst of it," Van Dorn added. "He

demanded we buy his extra horses, which we did, and then he demanded we pay him money in advance for goods he would bring from Bent's Fort."

"And you paid him?" Fritz asked quietly.

All the men looked down sheepishly. Van Dorn nodded. "We paid him," he admitted, with obvious bitterness in his voice. "He said that if we did not, he would bring the Utes down on us."

"He scared you out of your damned pants," Peaches concluded, with disgust.

"Ya, we were afraid," said Dieter. "He was looking at our wives and daughters when he said these things."

"He might do it, too," Fritz said. "I think he's in thick with the Utes."

"What do you mean?" Hans asked, suddenly even more interested in the two men he had almost left out to freeze to death in the cold.

"There was something fishy about Cleel gettin' a bunch of prospectors and trappers together and takin' them up in the mountains," Peaches explained. "We was ambushed and near 'bout everyone died."

"Is that why you are hunting him?" asked Van Dorn.

"He kilt my best friend."

"Maybe you can tell us what happened," Dieter said. The others nodded. Peaches recounted how Cleel had come to Cherry Creek and what happened after the prospectors on the South Platte were attacked. He told them of the expedition into the mountains and the two ambushes. Hans and the others listened in rapt silence as Maddy and Kris supplied everyone with hot cider and coffee.

"You are lucky you are alive," Van Dorn said. "My brother did not fare so well."

"How so?" Peaches asked.

"Young Pieter was always a hothead," Jan said. "He would not listen. He has—had," Jan corrected, "a wife and a little baby. He did not like John Cleel's threats and he took a pistol and was going to either shoot John or run him off."

"I remember Pieter," Kris said. Maddy nodded. She was carrying a tray of hot biscuits and had stopped to listen.

"Pieter, he told John to leave and not threaten us," Jan continued. "John told him to go and get him a sugar teat. Pieter drew his pistol and John shot him. Shot him dead."

"Right through the heart," Dieter said.

"And none of you did anything?" Fritz asked.

"I tried to rush him," Jan said, "but my friends held me back."

"We saved your life, Jan," a man named Lucius Fuhrmann put in.

"What happened then?" Peaches asked. "After your brother fell?"

Jan took a deep breath before he spoke. Firelight cast his eyes in deep shadows and etched his bearded face with flickers of flame. The silence stretched into each man's thoughts, sobered them as they waited for the reply many of them already knew.

"He took my brother's wife into their home," Jan said. "We could hear her screams as he attacked her. It was horrible. When he came out, it was very quiet in the house."

"Cleel laughed," Dieter said, his eyes wet with tears. "He laughed at all of us."

"And, then?" Fritz ventured.

"And then Cleel said he was coming back here to claim what was his," Jan said.

"What did he mean by that?" Peaches asked.

"I think he meant his daughter. That's why we rode out here, Hans. To warn you. To warn you that Cleel was coming."

"His daughter?" Hans repeated dumbly.

"I mean Sheila Stewart," Jan clarified. "Did you not know?"

"Cleel sold Sheila to us as a bondservant. That is, he was the broker. Maddy and I dealt with Sheila's mother."

"Cleel's wife, you mean," Jan said.

"His wife?" Maddy looked dumbstruck as she entered the circle of men. Light was beginning to spread over the eastern horizon like cream. It had long since stopped snowing, but no one there by the fire had noticed it.

"John Cleel. His real name is John Cleel Stewart," Dieter said.

"He told you this?" Hans asked.

"We knew it in St. Louis," Jan said. "Some of us."

"Why didn't you tell us?" Maddy demanded.

Jan hung his head. "We thought you knew."

Hans looked stunned. All were silent for a moment as the sun began to rise over the eastern horizon. Kris brought the pot of stew his mother had fixed and set it on the ground near the fire. Men picked up bowls and dipped from it with the ladle stuck inside, passing the pot around.

Fritz looked at the horizon. "Peaches," he said. "I'm going to look for Davey."

"You be careful crossing the Platte," Peaches cautioned.

"I know a place," was Fritz' cryptic reply. He went to the barn and saddled up his horse. By the time he rode out, the sun was well up in the sky and the men were still talking by the fire.

"When do you think Cleel will get here?" Peaches asked. He was looking at Van Dorn.

Jan shrugged. "A week, two."

"How so?" Peaches asked.

"He headed for Bent's Fort," Dieter said. "He'll be a month or more getting back."

Hans seemed relieved to hear this. He actually tried to smile, but the worry lines lingered on his forehead like the tracks of snakes.

"Maybe he only wanted us to think he was going to

Bent's Fort," Van Dorn suggested, and some of the men nodded in assent.

Peaches said nothing, but he finished his pipe and knocked out the dottle on a log, put it back in his possibles pouch. He got up from his squat by the fire and walked away, toward the barn.

"Reckon he's leavin', too," Dieter said.

Hans looked at Peaches' back, his face a study in confusion. Maddy turned toward her husband. "Maybe you should ask him to stay," she said softly.

"Why?" Hans asked.

"Because he said he was going to kill John Cleel."

"Oh, that's just talk," Hans scoffed, but his words did not carry the weight of conviction.

"We cannot stay long," Van Dorn said. "We must get back to our families and our farms."

"Why did so many of you come?" Hans wanted to know.

"We thought Cleel might have come here and killed you," Van Dorn replied.

"We wanted to help you if you needed it," Dieter added. "We wanted to fight Cleel if he was here."

Hearing these words, Maddy started to weep. She wiped her eyes, but the tears still welled up. Hans seemed to be choking on something; he was speechless.

No one spoke for several moments.

Finally Hans cleared his throat and started talking. "You all go on back. We don't need you. I will take care of Cleel if he comes back."

"You do not want our help?" Van Dorn asked.

"No," replied Hans. "Go when you are ready." He arose from his chair and walked up the steps and into the house. Maddy looked after him, a sad look in her eyes.

"He is a stubborn man," she said.

"Yes," Van Dorn agreed. "We will leave right away. This

little snow will melt quickly. It will be good for the seeds."
Several of the men grunted in agreement and they began to
leave the fire one by one. Maddy watched them, then turned
and walked to the steps. Kris still stood by the fire, staring into
it blankly.

"You help our friends," Maddy told him.

"Yes'm."

"And keep your rifle ready."

"He's going to come back, isn't he, Mama?"

"Cleel? Yes, he will be back."

"I—I don't know if I can kill a man."

"Your father can. And so can you, my son."

Kris's lips trembled. His mother, unable to witness the
fear in her son, slowly climbed up the steps and disappeared
inside the house.

When she entered the bedroom, Hans was sitting on the
edge of their bed, holding his head in his hands. He, too, was
weeping. She walked to him and put a hand on his back.

"Are you afraid?" she asked.

"Yes," Hans answered. "I've never been more afraid in
my life."

And they both heard the creak of leather and the rattle
of harnesses as the men from the settlement rode away,
leaving them all alone.

"That damned Sheila," Hans said. "We should never
have—"

"I know, my husband, I know," Maddy whispered sadly.
"Now we must make the best of it."

Hans stood up, looked at his wife. She started to cry
again.

"I won't let him hurt you," Hans swore.

Maddy nodded. "Do not worry, my husband."

"We will wait for him. Bring me my rifle."

The house seemed empty as she walked into the next
room. She went to the kitchen and picked up her husband's

rifle. Then she looked out the window that faced onto the South Platte and the mountains.

And there, riding toward the house, was the Arapaho, Eagle Heart, and Sheila sitting behind him on the spotted pony. Maddy's heart seemed to stop and her blood felt as hard as a frozen stone.

Chapter
Thirty-Seven

Davey hesitated, wondering whether he should follow the mule deer's tracks or simply give it up, letting the Ute, whose tracks were plain to see, make the kill. Something inside him rebelled at the thought. He had been tracking the deer first. But the Ute could not know that, of course, he reasoned.

He heard a noise and the decision was taken out of his hands. He saw the deer running, an arrow in its side, blood streaming from its wound. The muley turned, headed straight for him, then picked up his scent and veered away.

But then the animal stumbled and skidded through a patch of melting snow. It managed to get up again and Davey knew it might escape if he didn't fire his rifle. He took aim, led the deer, and squeezed off the shot. The crack of the rifle sounded alien to his ears after such a long silence. A puff of white smoke billowed from the barrel of his rifle and blended into near invisibility against the snow. He heard the ball strike hide and flesh.

The deer went down, its forelegs collapsing, then its haunches twisted and its rear went down, too. As the smoke cleared away, Davey quickly reloaded. Before he could walk to the deer, a Ute buck stepped out of a grove of aspen, an arrow nocked to his bowstring.

Davey set the butt of his rifle into the snow, leaned the barrel against his leg. Then he held up his left hand, palm out, to show that it was open, weaponless, and that he wanted to be a friend, not an enemy. The Ute looked at him for a long moment, then spoke in his native tongue.

Davey shook his head to show that he did not understand.

"Amigo," the Ute said.

Davey replied in English. "I am a friend, yes."

"You shot my deer."

"I stopped the deer. It was running away from you."

"Clear," the Ute said in Spanish. "Do you want the deer? It is mine."

"No. I am hungry, but the deer is yours."

The Ute smiled. He stepped out of the trees and walked slowly toward the dead deer.

"I will cut the deer's heart from its body and eat it," the Ute said. "I will cut you off a leg."

"That would please me."

"I am called Yellow Moon."

"I am called Davey."

The Ute laughed. "We call you Lynx."

"Why?" Davey asked.

"Because we have seen you catching the beaver and the deer. Because you hunt alone."

"I hunt alone," Davey acknowledged.

"Good. Take some of this meat and walk with the Great Spirit in peace."

"I will do that, Yellow Moon."

Davey kept his distance as the Ute skinned out the deer and quartered it. He wrapped his meat in the hide and left a hindquarter in the snow for Davey.

"Where do you go?" the trapper asked as the Ute started to walk back into the timber.

"I, too, hunt alone. I am not of the tribe anymore."

"Banished?" Davey asked, in Spanish.

"I do not know that Spanish word."

"Sent away."

"Yes."

"I will not ask why."

"No, it is not a good thing to know. Take care, Lynx."

"Take care yourself, Yellow Moon."

Davey waited until the Ute had gone and it was quiet again. Then he retrieved the hindquarter of the deer and carried it back to his camp. He slept in his blankets, and when he awoke, he built a fire and cut chunks of meat from the deer leg. He had some flour and salt, a small piece of dried onion. He trimmed fat from the leg and placed it in a skillet. Then he braised the meat and added the other ingredients, along with water from the Poudre. He set the skillet off from the full heat of the fire, on a stone, and let it simmer while his belly growled with hunger.

The snow was melting quickly under the sun and yet the air was still chill in the mountains. Davey put on his coat and checked his rifle and pistol. He gathered more wood for the evening fire, and when he returned, he saw a lone man on a horse riding up the canyon.

"Davey," Fritz called.

"Fritz. Come on up. I have some deer."

"I can smell it," Fritz said. "And I'm hungry."

"There's plenty."

Fritz rode up and dismounted. He hobbled his horse and set him to feed at the end of a long tether some distance from Davey's horse and mule. Neither man spoke again until Fritz returned to the campfire with his bedroll and some foodstuffs.

"I have a pair of potatoes and some fatback," Fritz said.

"That will do it. Do you have coffee?"

"I do."

As Davey added the fatback to the skillet Fritz brought

mud from the riverbank. They encased the potatoes in mud and put them on the edge of the fire in the hot coals.

"I could bring my skillet and make some bannock," Fritz offered.

"We'll get fat," Davey said. "What brings you up here?"

"I have news from Gwaltney," Fritz answered. "And I saw Eagle Heart and that Sheila girl down on the Platte."

"You're just bustin' to tell it all."

Fritz had met Eagle Heart when he and Davey had trapped together. Davey knew he had not seen Sheila until that day.

"Tell me what Bill Gwaltney has to say."

Fritz told Davey that the fur trade had gone under and that Gwaltney had returned to the fort. He also told him about the Groots and the settlers and the news that John Cleel was really John Cleel Stewart, Sheila's father.

"That bastard sold her into slavery."

"It looks that way. He's coming back, they say, to get her from the Groots. But he won't do it."

"No? Why not?"

"Eagle Heart says he will buy Sheila from the Groots and take her to his camp, to his blankets."

"And what does Sheila say about that?"

"She wants to go with him. She does not know about her father."

"You didn't tell her?"

"No. She has enough trouble, I'm thinking."

"Yes," Davey said. "Did Eagle Heart return Sheila to the Groots?"

"He said he was going to do that."

"You know, Fritz," Davey went on, "I don't think Sheila is for the Groots to sell. I don't think they have a bond on her any longer."

"No? Well, what about Cleel? Or Stewart, as it turns out to be."

"As far as I'm concerned, he gave up his right to claim his daughter the minute he sold her into bondage."

"Well, none of our business, eh?"

Davey's eyes narrowed. He breathed deep of the alpine air. He thought about Sheila, his feelings for her. Maybe it was none of his business, but he had felt a strong tug at his heart when he had found the cave empty. He missed her. Maybe he even loved her.

"Fritz," Davey started, "I think it *is* our business. Mine, anyway. If Sheila goes with Eagle Heart, she'll be a slave with the Arapahos, just as she has been with the Groots. You know how they treat captives."

"But she ain't no captive if Eagle Heart trades for her."

"No, she will be. And I'm not going to let it happen."

"Damn, Davey, you puzzle me. Hell, someone might think you're in love with that girl."

Davey looked hard and long at his old partner as the firelight danced shadows on his face.

"Well, Fritz, maybe I am. Yes, maybe I do love Sheila. And tomorrow I'm going to take her from the Groots—by force, if necessary."

"And then what will you do with her, son?"

"I'll marry her, if she'll have me."

And the moment he said it, Davey knew that he truly loved Sheila and would fight for her.

Chapter
Thirty-Eight

Peaches watched as Eagle Heart rode away from the Groot homestead. The brave had promised he would return with ponies and fresh meat and buy Sheila from Hans. It seemed to him that Hans couldn't wait to get rid of the girl before John Cleel returned. And Maddy, too. The only one who didn't seem pleased was their son, Kris.

"I hope he comes back soon," Maddy said.

"Me, too," Hans agreed.

Peaches looked at the house and down toward the river, then to the place where the Poudre flowed into the South Platte.

"What do you look at?" Hans asked.

"I just wondered if Davey ever said anything to you about putting your homestead here."

"He did," Hans confirmed.

"Not a good place to put down roots," Peaches said. "This here's a buffalo trail and the Injuns use it like a highway. And you're right smack-dab in the middle of it."

"Well, here we will stay," Hans said stubbornly.

"Suit yourself." Peaches shrugged.

The three of them walked into the house after they could no longer see Eagle Heart. Kris and Sheila were tending to the chores. Peaches and Kris had put out the fire that had burned through the night.

Inside the house, Hans paced the front room nervously before coming to a stop by a small boarded-up window to peer through a gun port to the east.

"You won't see him when he comes," Peaches told him.

"He has to come across the wide-open spaces," Hans said.

Maddy left the room, walking softly so she could still hear the conversation.

"He'll come in a way so's you can't see him."

"Well, if he comes now, he can take Sheila, damn her."

"That might not be all he'll take," Peaches said.

"What do you mean by that?"

"He might take your life," Peaches replied.

"My God," Hans breathed.

Peaches stood next to the front window. The snow that had fallen during the night was almost gone and there was no wind. Everything seemed peaceful and serene. But his heart was pounding out of control as he thought of the waiting ahead. Cleel could come at any time, but he didn't expect him to show up in broad daylight. Cleel was too smart for that.

But he might come today. Cleel was that bold. Arrogant, even.

Peaches thought of the men who had been slaughtered in the mountains, of Tall Tom and the way he died. There was something rotten in a man like Cleel, a man who would sell his own daughter and rob the dead.

A man like that did not deserve to live.

But Cleel was like a worm. You could cut him to pieces and he'd grow new parts. The only way to get rid of such a man was to stomp him into the dirt, smash him senseless so that he could never hurt anyone again.

Peaches turned away from the window.

He hated the waiting.

Chapter Thirty-Nine

Sheila finished gathering the eggs from the henhouse and cleaning out the nest. As she was turning away from the last nest, a shadow filled the doorway.

"Had yourself a time with them fellers, didn't you?" Kris asked.

"I don't know what you mean, Kris." Suddenly Sheila was afraid.

Kris smiled knowlingly. The smile was very close to an outright smirk.

"Sure you do, Sheila. Davey, he took you up into the hills, and then you come back with that buck."

"Davey is lost. He might be dead."

"The Injun kill him?"

"How dare you say such a thing?"

"Well, Eagle Heart said he was agoin' to buy you from Papa. You must have given him some reason."

"I never," she said, her face flushing a bright pink.

"Maybe I'll help me to some of what they got," Kris said.

Sheila set down the basket of eggs, glared at Kris. He moved inside the henhouse.

"You come any closer, Kris," she warned, "I'll scream."

"Hell, I don't mind a little screamin', Sheila."

He took another step toward her.

Suddenly she flew at him like a tigress, clawing and scratching at his face. She pushed on his chest and drove him backward, out the door. She kicked him in the genitals and he doubled up in pain, but did not utter a cry.

"You leave me alone, Kris Groot, or I'll tear your eyes out."

Kris held his hands over his groin. He was bent over, grimacing, as Sheila turned and went back inside the henhouse to get the basket of eggs. When she came back outside, Kris was dusting himself off.

"It's a good thing you're goin' away with that Injun," he said. "Or you'd pay for what you done to me."

She glared at him, her eyes wild. "You're more savage than Eagle Heart."

"Don't be callin' me no names, neither," Kris said.

"There aren't any names for someone like you," she spat, and stalked off toward the house. She felt dirty and it was all she could do to stem the tide of tears that welled up in her eyes.

She stopped before going inside the house and wiped her eyes.

All of a sudden she felt that the whole world was against her. She had thought she might ride off with Eagle Heart and live with his people as an Arapaho, but he was determined to pay for her. While she admired his sense of honor, she also felt abandoned by him. If Davey were alive, she realized, she might beseech him to take her away from the Groots.

But now she was all alone, and sure that the Groots now hated her more than ever. Maddy had probably put Kris up to going after her, raping her, and making her no good for any man.

Deep inside, Sheila was terrified. There was no one she could turn to, no one who could help her. She drew in a deep breath and climbed up the steps.

Peaches and Hans were in the front room, their rifles near at hand. She did not look at them as she walked to the kitchen. Maddy was by the stove, fixing more stew, she supposed.

"What took you so long?" the older woman asked, her words like a lash across Sheila's face.

"Your son came after me," Sheila answered. "As if you didn't know."

Maddy turned and glared savagely at the girl.

"You shut your filthy mouth. Kris did no such thing."

"No, well, why don't you ask him? It's not the first time, you know."

"Sheila, I ought to beat you within an inch of your life. Talking like that. You ungrateful slut."

Sheila set the basket of eggs on the table and stood defiantly, her jaw set, her fists clenched.

"You've beaten me for the last time, Maddy. I'm not afraid of you anymore. And I'm not afraid of Hans or Kris, either."

Maddy started to stalk toward her, but was stopped by the look in the girl's eyes.

"You've become like that savage you were with," Maddy said.

"No, Maddy, I haven't. You're the savage. Eagle Heart has more manners than any of you and he knows what kindness is."

"How dare you say such things to me? I've been like a mother to you," Maddy said angrily.

"A mother? You couldn't hold a candle to my mother, Maddy."

"Your mother, Sheila? She sold you to us, remember? And now your father is coming to get you."

Sheila gasped in surprise. "My father? What do you mean?"

"I mean your father made your mother sell your servitude to us, and now he wants you back."

"You're lying," Sheila cried, but even as she said it she knew Maddy's words must be true. It was one more whip across her back, one more cruelty life had dealt her. She felt faint. Her knees began to buckle. The room started to spin and then went black.

Chapter Forty

Fritz Stamm awoke to a familiar smell. He shaded his eyes from the rising sun as he sat up on his bedroll to look around. Stacks of prime furs lay on the ground within a few feet of him. Davey was placing a rack on the back of his mule, hitching it up tight.

"What the hell you doing, Davey?" Fritz asked.

"Repacking the mule."

"Those furs from your cache?"

"Uh-huh."

"What the hell for? I told you what Bill Gwaltney said."

"I know. But it seems a shame to have killed all these animals for nothing. So I'm takin' them down the mountain."

"You can't sell 'em."

"No, Fritz, I can't. But I can give them to Eagle Heart. The Indians can make purses, pouches, water bags, and whatnot from 'em."

Fritz crabbed from his blankets and stood up, scratching his head, rubbing the sleep from his eyes. He stretched and extended his arms toward the sun.

"You wouldn't be wanting to bribe Eagle Heart, would you?" he asked.

"No, it's not that. Let be what will be, Fritz."

"Haw! That ain't you, Davey."

"I would like to see her again. Ask her if that's what she wants."

"You don't think she wants to marry up with Eagle Heart?"

"I don't really know," Davey said. "But I'd like to know if the choice is hers. I'm thinkin' she'd do anything to get away from those Groots."

"They ain't a family you can warm up to much."

"No," Davey acknowledged.

The two men finished filling the panniers and rigging slings for the fur packets on Davey's mule and their two horses. Shortly before noon, they started down Poudre Canyon. The sun was still shining bright and the snow was almost completely melted. Six hours later they reached the Platte, which was running smooth and calm, but full.

They saw the Groot place on the knoll, smoke rising from its chimney. Neither man had a glass to see the house close up, but people were moving around, and everything seemed normal.

"Where do you want to ford, Davey?"

"Down aways, I think. River takes a bend, widens out. Should be shallow enough for most of it, and we can swim what's left."

Fritz nodded.

Davey had started to turn his horse when some movement caught the corner of his eye. He shifted in the saddle and saw a patch of color on the northern horizon. "Look yonder, Fritz," he said.

The other man turned and peered in the direction toward which Davey was pointing.

"Hmm. What do you make of it, Davey?"

"Arapaho, I reckon. Take 'em a couple of hours to reach the Groot homestead. "They're movin' awful slow."

"A bunch of 'em, I'd say."

"C'mon, let's cross this damned river so we can be on the right side when they reach the Groots."

Davey rode to the wide bend in the South Platte and saw that the water had eaten away more of the banks and that the river was fairly shallow for most of the way. He could see the sandbars in the middle, so he knew it was not very deep there. The water was racing at a pretty good pace, but was not too swift to bowl over the horses and mule.

He found a low part of the bank and put his horse in, pulling on the mule's rope. The mule balked, but as the horse struck the water and forged ahead, the mule finally slid down the bank, bracing itself with all four hooves.

Fritz followed soon after, and they made the ford with no difficulty. The horse under Davey scrambled up the opposite bank and the mule did not falter. Fritz joined him a few seconds later.

"Where to, Davey? The house?"

"The house. Might prove interesting."

"To say the least," Fritz commented.

Within fifteen minutes Davey rode up in full sight of the house. He saw no signs of life. Then a man appeared on the porch. It was not Groot.

"That's old Peaches, wouldn't you know?" Fritz said.

"Why, damned if it ain't," Davey agreed.

Peaches waved to them, and Fritz waved back. Davey's stomach was churning like a boiling spring. "Where in hell are the Groots?" he asked.

"Probably inside, their rifles trained on both of us," Fritz guessed.

"I'm damned surprised Peaches is there. Hans Groot sure as hell doesn't like company."

"I know," Fritz said. "But it looks like he's goin' to have a hell of a lot right soon. Looky yonder."

Fritz pointed off to the east. There, just clearing the horizon, was a wagon, drawn by two horses, another horse in tow. A man sat on the buckboard seat, striking the rumps of the horses with a thin whip. The horses were trotting, trying to break into a gallop.

"Hell of a way to treat good horseflesh," Davey grumbled. "Is that old man Groot?"

"No, but he looks mighty familiar."

When Davey looked back at the house, Peaches had disappeared. There was an odd silence about the homestead now, with not a soul in sight.

Davey looked again at the wagon. The horses were now in full gallop, the wagon jouncing over the plowed fields like an out-of-control ship on a stormy sea.

"You know who the hell that is?" Fritz asked, a tone of incredulity in his voice.

Davey looked again. The man stood up, still whipping the horse. He was in a hell of a hurry, the trapper thought.

"It can't be," he said. "Can it?"

"It damned sure looks like John Cleel."

And Davey knew that Fritz was right as the man in the wagon sat back down on the seat.

So it was true, he thought. Cleel was coming back to claim his daughter. And Peaches was bound to kill him.

Davey's stomach tightened into a hard knot. There would be blood spilled this afternoon, he figured. He wondered why Cleel would come to the Groots all alone when he must have known there would be a fight.

"Come on, Fritz," he shouted, touching his heels to his horse's flanks. "Let's get up to the house before Cleel gets there."

Fritz needed no urging; he kicked his horse into a gallop, right on Davey's heels.

Chapter

Forty-One

Peaches ran into the front room and grabbed up his rifle. Hans, who had been dozing in a chair near the window, sat up instantly, his face blanching to a colorless paste. "What is it?" he asked.

"John Cleel is acomin', hell-bent for leather, and he's pullin' a wagon."

Sheila came running out of the kitchen, followed by Maddy. Both looked terrified. "Kris, where is Kris?" Maddy shouted.

Hans grabbed his rifle from its place against the wall, hastily checked the powder in the pan. "I—I don't know. In the barn, I think."

Peaches ran out onto the porch and was down the steps before anyone in the house knew he had left.

He stared at the onrushing wagon in amazement. Behind it, he saw something more ominous, more puzzling. Off in the distance a huge cloud of dust billowed toward the sky, a reddish dust such as he had never seen before. The cloud threatened to block out the sun as it expanded and rose ever higher.

Peaches stood there, hypnotized. He heard a faint voice yelling and realized that it was Cleel himself. He was shouting something that Peaches could not make out.

He turned as Davey and Fritz rode up at a breakneck gallop. They, too, were looking toward the east, not at Cleel in the wagon, but at the huge cloud of red dust that was growing larger by the minute.

"Anyone in the house?" Davey asked as he swung down out of the saddle.

"Everyone, except Kris."

"Keep 'em in there."

"What the hell's goin' on?" Peaches asked.

"Buffalo," Davey said, panting for a breath. "Right on Cleel's backside."

Peaches swore a muffled oath and turned toward the house. That's when he saw the Arapaho break ranks and ride to the east, striking a path that would bring them right along the onrushing buffalo herd.

"Fritz," Davey called, "let's get these horses and the mule in the barn. They might be safe there."

Fritz needed no urging. As Peaches scrambled up the front steps Davey started running toward the barn, pulling his horse and mule behind him.

The ground began to tremble and Davey heard the shrieking cries of the Arapaho as they raced to the hunt. Cleel was still a quarter mile away, but Davey could see the lather on the chests of both horses making up his team.

"He might make it," Fritz said.

"It'll be damned close," Davey replied.

Kris emerged from the barn as Davey and Fritz reached it. His face was white as flour. He clutched his rifle in his hands.

"What's goin' on?" the young man asked.

"Buffalo stampede," Davey said. "You'd better get in the house."

"Who's that comin' with the wagon?" Kris asked.

"John Cleel," Fritz told him. "And he's the least of your troubles."

Kris ran to the house as Davey pulled his horse and mule inside the barn. Fritz followed him in, sweating and panting.

"Just leave 'em, Fritz, and let's get the hell out of here."

"Reckon them buffalo will veer off and go somewhere else?"

"Not likely," Davey said. "They smell water and we're right in their path."

"Maybe them Injuns will break 'em up," Fritz suggested.

"You'd better hope to God."

Davey shut the barn doors and started toward the house.

Cleel rode up then, his horses staggering, their coats slick with sweat, their mouths foaming with creamy lather. He set the brake and the wagon ground to a halt. Cleel wrapped the reins around the brake and leaped to the ground, rifle in hand.

That's when Peaches came back outside and bounded down the steps, his rifle already coming to his shoulder.

"Don't come no closer, Cleel," he yelled. "I'm going to blow you straight to hell."

But Cleel's rifle was already to his shoulder and he was drawing a bead on the former trapper. Davey dropped to his knees and brought his own rifle to his shoulder, cocking the hammer as the barrel rose to bring Cleel into his sights.

It was then that Sheila rushed out onto the porch, screaming hysterically.

"Don't shoot him," she yelled.

Davey looked away for just a moment to see Sheila on the porch.

Shots rang out and the ground shook and they all could hear the roar of distant thunder as the buffalo herd broke over the eastern horizon.

Chapter
Forty-Two

Cleel fired his rifle at the same time as Peaches squeezed the trigger on his rifle. Twin clouds of smoke billowed from both muzzles. Peaches gasped and dropped his weapon as he staggered toward Sheila, his eyes fixed with horror.

John Cleel doubled over as the ball from Peaches' rifle struck him at his belt line. Blood spread from the wound, but the man remained standing.

"Fritz, see about Peaches, will you?" Davey asked. "And get Sheila inside the house."

"You bet," Fritz said, and ran toward the porch.

The thundering became louder as the buffalo herd began to fill the horizon. Dust streamed from the prairie as thousands of hooves broke up the soil, churning it to powder.

Davey got up and walked toward Cleel.

"Is—is my father hurt?" Sheila cried out. "Don't kill him, Davey. Please don't kill him."

The trapper snatched Cleel's rifle from his hands. Cleel glared at him, and began to feebly claw for the pistol in his belt.

"I'll drop you where you stand if you even touch that pistol," Davey warned him.

"Damn you, Longworth. I should have killed you at Cherry Creek."

"Well, you're done for, Cleel. That's a gut wound and you'll die slow and hard."

"I ain't finished yet. That buffalo herd's goin' to grind you and everybody else into the dirt."

Cleel began to laugh harshly.

Davey took Cleel's pistol from his belt. He wondered if he should just leave him there to die, or try to bring him into the house. Behind him, he heard Sheila protesting as Fritz tried to wrestle her inside the house.

The matter was taken out of Davey's hands as Sheila broke loose from Fritz and ran down the steps. In seconds she was standing beside Davey. Fritz knelt down to see how Peaches was doing. The wounded trapper's shirt was sodden with blood and he was breathing with difficulty.

"Are you my father?" Sheila asked, looking at John Cleel.

"What do you think?" Cleel snarled.

"I hate you for what you did to my mother."

"She warn't no good, gal. Just like you."

"No, you're no good," Sheila said.

Davey pulled the girl away from Cleel. "Sheila, that herd's going to run right over us if we don't get to the house. Come on, let's go."

"What about him?" she asked, looking at her father.

"What do you want me to do? Try to save him?"

"I—I don't know," she said, and hung her head.

A moment passed and Davey looked up, saw the buffalo fanning out. In a few minutes they would swarm over the Groot homestead, trampling everything in their path.

On the porch, Peaches whispered to Fritz. "Did I get him, Fritz?"

"No, Cleel's still alive."

"Kill him, Fritz. Kill him for me, will you?"

Fritz took a deep breath.

The stock in the barn began to scream and kick the walls with their hooves.

Davey grabbed Sheila and pushed her toward the house.

Fritz stood up and brought his rifle to his shoulder.

"Kill him," Peaches croaked.

Fritz took aim at Cleel now that Davey and Sheila were well away from him. He put the front blade sight right in the middle of Cleel's forehead. He had never killed a man before, and his hands started to shake.

"Shoot him," Peaches whispered in a husky voice.

Fritz sucked in a breath and held it. The wavering barrel steadied and the sight held tight on Cleel's forehead. The old trapper squeezed the trigger and the rifle bucked against his shoulder as sparks flew from the pan through the touch hole and ignited the powder in the barrel.

Davey and Sheila stopped for a second and looked back.

Fritz's lead ball struck Cleel in the forehead, just above the bridge of his nose. The back of his head blew apart, scattering pieces of skull and brain matter in a rosy spray. Cleel's eyes opened wide and his mouth gaped, but he was dead before he hit the ground.

Sheila gasped and put a fist to her mouth.

Davey jerked her away from the grisly sight and shoved her ahead of him.

"Did you get him, Fritz?" Peaches asked, his voice faint.

"I got him, Peaches."

"Good," the former trapper said. Then he closed his eyes and let out a breath. It was his last.

Tears welled up in Fritz's eyes as he brought his rifle down and mechanically began to reload it with powder and ball.

"Here they come," Davey yelled as he and Sheila reached the bottom step of the porch.

"Peaches done died," Fritz said as Davey and Sheila scrambled up the steps.

"Leave him be and go on in the house," Davey told him.

Inside, everyone crowded the front room, peering through the windows and gun ports. In seconds the herd roared past the house, streaming on both sides of it like a river of dark brown wool. The roar was so loud it drowned out all other sound.

Sheila snuggled into Davey's arms. She was trembling, but her eyes were dry.

The herd took the better part of an hour to reach the river, and then it was quiet, with only occasional whoops from the Arapaho in the distance as they finished off wounded animals.

Davey and Sheila stepped outside. Where Cleel had fallen there were only rags and scraps of his boots. The wagon was just boards and iron and the pair of horses were nowhere to be seen.

"Davey, I don't want to go with Eagle Heart. But I don't want to stay here, either."

"Will you come with me?" he asked.

"Where are you going?"

"I don't know. West. Away from here."

"I'll go with you, Davey. Anywhere."

Davey squeezed her tightly and she looked up at him, offering her lips. He leaned down and kissed her.

"Take me with you now," she said. "The sooner the better."

"No good-byes?"

"No good-byes. I said them all when I was in the mountains."

Davey smiled. He gave her another squeeze, then walked to the barn, hand in hand with Sheila. The barn still stood and the horses and mules were all right.

At the end of an hour Davey had two horses saddled, his own and Peaches'. He had instructed Fritz to give his furs to Eagle Heart.

"So long, Davey," Fritz said. The Groots had gone out to look at their fields, which had been destroyed by the buffalo stampede. They were still out there, watching the Arapaho women as they swarmed over the dead buffalo, butchering them with sharp knives.

"So long, Fritz. Did you recognize that wagon Cleel drove up?"

"No, can't say as I did. Why?"

"You've seen it before," Davey said. "At Cherry Creek."

Fritz thought about it for a minute. He scratched his head, then his eyes opened wide. "Well, I'll be damned. It is true?"

"It is," Davey said. "That was Bill Gwaltney's wagon. I'll bet Bill's money is scattered from hell to breakfast after those buffalo ran through here. Cleel's pockets were full of stolen money."

"And he probably cached the furs Bill bought from us somewhere."

"My father was no good," Sheila whispered.

"If he really was your father," Davey said. "I have my doubts."

Sheila looked dubious for a moment, then her face broke out in a smile.

"Davey," she said, laughingly, "you always know the right thing to say."

Davey touched the brim of his hat in a salute of farewell to his old partner. Sheila waved good-bye to the old trapper.

"Be seein' you, Davey," Fritz said. "Maybe in Californy."

Davey said nothing. There was a lot of country to the west and he wanted to see it all. He wanted Sheila to see it, too. When they found the place they were looking for, they would know it. It would be a place where they could both start fresh and build a life that had no shadows in it, no skeletons from the past.

At the top of a rise, he stopped and looked down at the South Platte river, shimmering silver in the sunlight.

"Beautiful river," he said.

"Yes," Sheila breathed.

"It holds many secrets."

"And carries them all away to the sea," Sheila said.

Davey laughed. He knew he had found himself a right smart woman.

About the Author

JORY SHERMAN is the Spur Award–winning author of *The Medicine Horn, Song of the Cheyenne, Horne's Law, Winter of the Wolf,* and *Grass Kingdom.* In addition to *The South Platte,* he has written *The Arkansas River, The Rio Grande,* and *The Columbia River* for Bantam's Rivers West series. His next novel in the series, *The Brazos River,* will be published in 1999. He currently resides with his wife near Belton, Texas.

If you enjoyed Jory Sherman's epic tale, *The South Platte,* be sure to look for the next installment of the Rivers West saga at your local bookstore. Each new volume takes you on a voyage of exploration along one of the great rivers of North America with the courageous pioneers who challenged the unknown.

Rivers West

THE CIMARRON RIVER

by

Gary McCarthy

*On sale in spring 1999 wherever
Bantam Books are sold*